£9.95

F.

OLLEGE

D1324739

Eighteen Vagabond Eighteen

Sheep and Goats

by
Lewis Gordon

Vagabond Voices
Glasgow

First published in September 2014 by
Vagabond Voices Publishing Ltd.,
Glasgow,
Scotland.

ISBN 978-1-908251-33-6

Printed and bound in Poland

Cover design by Mark Mechan

Typeset by Park Productions

The publisher acknowledges subsidy towards
this publication from Creative Scotland

For further information on Vagabond Voices, see the website,
www.vagabondvoices.co.uk

For Kirsty

And thanks to Allan Cameron, Alan McMunnigall, Brian Hamill and Neil Gordon for wisdom, guidance, encouragement, and to my folks for everything

Sheep and Goats

Sixth-Year Girls

Pete was waiting there, kicking at a stone jammed in the tar.

"How come you're always late?"

Nicky pulled up his sleeve and went to say something.

"Look," Pete nodded down the road. Two girls from sixth year were crossing. "Come on."

They walked down the hill to the main road, the pavement crammed with groups in uniform.

"Good weekend?" Pete said.

Nicky shrugged.

Pete made a long step, dodging some trodden-in dogshit. "My brother's mates were over. We got a few beers in. Sunday's hangover was a bastard."

Shoving past some kids from first year, they fell in behind the two girls. One wore a skirt just above her knees and the other's was shorter and tight around her bigger thighs. She walked with one foot turning inward. You could see the heel of her shoe worn squint.

"Which one, Nick? Left or right?"

"I dunno."

"Give us a straight answer for once."

"They can hear you."

"Definitely the left."

"I'm not sure."

"You like them chunky?"

"I wouldn't call her chunky."

"You've got a fat fetish."

"They can hear you."

"Not saying I wouldn't, she's still a big ride. I just like blondes more."

The dark-haired girl turned, flicked her hair and faced forward.

"I love it when they wear those shiny tights," Pete said, "Or no tights at all."

They slowed down, keeping the same distance the whole way.

When they arrived it was early and Pete made them go across to the newsagents. He bought a roll and a packet of crisps, and handed his money to the miserable old woman. Outside he said, "I hate having to touch her hands. Fuckin' dry and horrible."

They walked towards the gates, eyes away from the smokers on the wall outside the shop. Pete nodded ahead. "Jennifer Black's coming."

She came towards them on her skinny legs, arms folded tight, her chubby pal unwrapping a packet of cigarettes. Jennifer Black's hair fell straight to her jaw, cut at an angle matching the sharp line of her face.

"Awright Jennifer?" Pete said.

"Awright Skelf." The girls pushed in-between, heading for the smokers.

"See yous," Pete said. He walked a few steps with his neck twisted.

Nicky had been put next to her in art once. Her

shirt had been rumpled and he'd seen though a gap in the buttons to the white bra underneath.

They met up again at lunch and went over to the usual bit at the fence.

"See much of your pal at the weekend?" Pete said.

"Who?"

"Wee cock-tease."

Nicky didn't answer.

"Is that a yes? You finally get her nailed?"

"I didn't see her."

"I told you what my brother says. Private school girls get them down easy."

"She has to wear one of those long skirts."

"Yeah. But when they're not in school, I mean," he spat on the playground. "She's a bible-basher anyway, isn't she?"

Nicky shrugged.

"Does that mean you'll both be big virgins till you get married?"

"She's just a mate."

"I'm your mate too. You're not trying to ride me."

Pete built another roll and crisps while Nicky stuffed his sandwiches down. They watched the mob boot a manky tennis ball about. He looked at his watch and said, "I'm away to that concert."

"When?"

"Now. This lunchtime."

"The thing all they gay posters are about?"

"You coming?" Nicky said.

"No chance."

"Might be better than hanging about here for once."

"It'll be mosher shite."

"Mibbe." He pulled his bag on both shoulders and started walking, "Sure you don't want to go?"

Pete shook his head then turned away to someone else. Nicky tightened his bag straps and kept going.

There was a chair in the back row, far enough away from the rest of them. They were huddled near the stage, long leather coats and army jackets over their uniforms. Pete had christened one of the girls the Nazi Witch. She was there in her big black boots.

The curtains squeaked. A boy with spiked hair was waiting, holding a guitar. There were slow claps and whistles, and he stepped to the microphone, strummed and opened his mouth. He had something to say, he sang. The bass and drums went BAM BAM. Then he sang a line about killing someone's baby.

The boy's arm stabbed at the guitar strings and the beat began. There was a bass player, frowning at the notes through his black hair with a tie from another school slack round his neck. The drummer blinked hard every time he hit his kick drum, moving his lips with the words.

Before the first verse was done, Granny D the music teacher marched on, hand slashing across her throat. A curtain followed her across the stage. The other came from the opposite side, closing over the band. They stopped. You could hear their voices spilling over the speakers.

"We talked about this. Nothing obscene, I said."

"I didn't swear."

"You know very well it was inappropriate. That

song." Granny D tutted. "I went to a lot of trouble for this."

Someone at the front booed.

"You abused my trust," she said.

She began telling them to pack their things. Three clicks sounded and the band started up again. The curtains shook. The guitar clanged off something and turned to screeching, and folk covered their ears. Behind the curtains something was going on, making them flap and billow. There was a thud. The microphone rolled off the stage and hung by the wire. Granny D's foot appeared, shoe dangling and dropping in to the hall. A long-haired boy picked it up and slid it inside his trench coat.

"SHUT UP THIS INSTANT," Granny D yelled. The foot vanished.

They'd shut off the speakers, but they couldn't stop the drummer.

"Think he'll get expelled?" Pete said.

"Dunno. Someone said he got suspended before."

"Daft fuckin' moshers."

"You should've come."

"To hear some freak singing about raping a baby for ten seconds?"

"It wasn't that."

"Whatever. The guy's a sicko."

They stopped outside Nicky's.

"Mine for a bit of playstation?" Pete said.

"I'm going in."

"Scared you'll get beat again?"

"I've got stuff to do."

Pete shrugged. "Fine. See you later." He walked off.

Inside, Nicky dumped his stuff, then unhooked the hatch to the loft. The stairs slid out and he climbed towards his drums.

Ruth was at the other end of the couch. Whenever she moved, her perfume wafted over. The film ended and Nicky watched a tear drip down her cheek.

"You knew that was going to happen," he said.

"It's still sad though. Remember at the cinema? I was a total mess."

She slid along the couch until their shoulders were touching.

"Does it not annoy you, how everything goes wrong every two minutes?" Nicky said.

"It's a film. It'd be boring otherwise."

"At least it'd be over quicker."

She sighed. "Fine. You can pick next time."

Ruth sniffed and examined a few strands of her hair. She got up and stuck on a CD and went back to the far end of the couch. It was the Counting Crows album and they didn't speak for the first song. Everything was pristine in her house. On the opposite wall there was a family portrait – Ruth, her wee brother and her parents with fake grins on their faces. It was from a few years ago, when she was still flat-chested.

Nicky spoke eventually. "Thanks for having me over."

"Are you done moaning?"

"I was just kidding."

She looked away.

"Sorry," he said.

Her feet brushed his thigh and tucked themselves under her. "It's fine. I'm just pissed off with mum and dad, making me stay in for the brat. Like I'm his private babysitter."

"You should get them to pay you."

"They say I'm earning my allowance."

She yawned and stretched flat so her legs lay on his. "When d'you need to go?"

"Just whenever."

She closed her eyes. "I'm shattered."

He nodded. He went to say something then closed his mouth and put his hands on her knees. Her eyes blinked open.

"I'll go then," he said and stood.

"I'm not trying to get rid of you."

"I know." He zipped up his jacket and went to the front door. "You going to youth club this week?"

"Mibbe."

"I'll see you on Sunday anyway."

"I hope so."

She gave him a tight hug and he left the house. It was dark and he had to edge along the pavement, past big four-by-fours and sports cars sitting tilted on the kerb. A stiffy was pushing hard against his fly, but as he walked it gradually eased off.

Sid

Mack tapped the white and it nudged another ball. It should've stopped, but rolled down the slope into a pocket. Bits of torn up cardboard were stacked under the rickety table legs.

"Jammy," Nicky said.

"Pure skill. I'm an old pro."

"You're just old."

Mack missed and the white trundled into the corner. Nicky had to lift the cue high, because the hall was too narrow. He sliced his shot.

"Two to me," Mack said. "You'll be my age before you know it, by the way."

"People are always saying that."

"Think about it bud. Every year is a smaller percentage of your life. It all starts going faster."

Some local kids came in to the church, shoving a door so it smacked the wall and plaster puffed out. "Watch it," Mack shouted. He went back to his shot. "We used to tear about our youth club like that lot. Drinking in the square before and causing ruckus," he missed his shot and tutted. "Now I'm running the show."

A rap song came on the stereo in the main hall. There were a couple of FUCKS in the first few lines. Mack stared down his cue. There was a loud

MOTHERFUCKER. He blinked, straightened and went next door. The music stopped.

Beside the pool table some wee kids were playing table tennis. One of them sent the ball bouncing high, off the ceiling and on the other side. The other boy missed, laughing hard and high pitched. The main door opened again, setting off the security buzzer. It was Mack, chucking an acne-faced boy out. He was trying to squirm out Mack's grip, saying, "I was going anyway. This place is a pure shitehole."

A new CD came on. It was the Counting Crows CD again.

When the red numbers said 23:03 he was still awake, scanning the TV channels. Outside there was arguing and laughter. Pulling back the curtain, he saw a group going down the street – a girl tightrope walking along the white road lines, leaping from one to the next. One of the boys swung a fat plastic bottle. The girl stopped, looked and Nicky dropped the curtain, peeking through the gap underneath, seeing her take a run and jump on the boy's back, then disappear round the corner.

Back on the bed, he tapped the remote again. All he was after was a pair of tits. More if he got lucky. Next to the alarm clock a load of toilet paper was scrunched up, ready. After a few more scrolls he muted the TV and closed his eyes.

The last thing he saw was Jennifer Black in the summer, stick-thin legs brown and bare and leaning over a desk. Her pants had flopped round her ankles. It was always women though – Pete told him that's how you found out if you were gay: if right before you came you couldn't help thinking of men.

He opened his eyes. It wasn't as bad this way. Doing it to the TV always made you feel worse, even though it was the same mess to clear up in the end.

Out in the congregation a few hands popped up like aerials. Nicky played a fast fill, smashing a cymbal. Janet Johnson was on the piano. She gave him a look over her music, a mound of grey hair springing on her head. Back when he first started playing at services, some old people had been upset. A few of them moved to another church.

When Nicky was dismantling the kit, the boy came down the aisle, eyes pointing at his black boots. His T-shirt showed a man smashing up a bass guitar. It was the boy with spiked hair. The singer.

He stopped and went, "Awright."

"Hi."

"You have to do that every week?"

"What?"

"Play all the songs?"

"Most weeks. They make me tidy it away though."

The boy nodded, hand coming up and pushing his earring around in its hole. Nicky started collapsing a cymbal stand.

"You're at my school, aren't you? Year below?" the boy said.

"Didn't know you came here."

"Stuck with my dad this week and he dragged me along. Old prick."

He grinned and Nicky put the flattened stand down.

"What sort of music you into?"

"I dunno. Anything," Nicky looked at him and shrugged. "Green Day."

The boy shook his head. "Green Day. Pretty shite. The Clash and the Stooges are better. That's proper punk."

Nicky reached for something then straightened and rubbed his hands on his khaki trousers.

"Listen. I just kicked the drummer out my band. We need someone new."

"I saw your concert the other day."

"Yeah? Granny D's such an arsehole." He held out a scrap of paper. "Come for an audition. My house after school tomorrow."

It was torn from the church notice sheet. Under the name SID there was an address and phone number and a skull and cross bones. When he looked up Sid was walking away. Folk hanging about the aisles with their tea and coffee turned to see him go.

Purdy

"You can make out arses better in trousers. With mine anyway." Pete nodded at the other girl. "Your one's are a bit baggy but. Shame."

Buttons on the blonde girl's back pockets peeked at them like doll's eyes.

Nicky said, "How come she's mine?"

"I told you I always go for the blondes."

"Jennifer Black's not a blonde."

"Aye she is. A bit."

"That's just a few stripes."

"What's colour's your pal got again?"

"Who?"

"The wee Bible-basher you're after."

"I'm not after her."

"My brother says there was this Christian girl in his year," Pete said. "Wasn't even good looking but everyone was after her cos she took it up the bum."

They walked to the newsagent without saying anything else.

While Pete was filling his roll with the crisps, Jennifer Black and her chubby friend appeared. He shoved the food in his pocket and said, "Morning Jennifer."

"Awright Skelf." They went to push by.

"Good weekend?" Pete said, "What d'you get up to?"

"What were you and your wee boyfriend up to?"

He gave Nicky a shove. "This poof'd be lucky to have me."

"We were at a party. Got shit-faced then Mark took us out in his car."

"Whose party?" Pete said.

Nicky caught the other girl's eye by mistake. She frowned, blowing smoke from her angry wee mouth.

Jennifer Black said, "Purdy's. Him and Barry were buzzing gas all night. Barry smacked his head off a shelf."

"Purdy," Pete said, "the man with a pie supper for a face."

Jennifer Black laughed then looked over at the wall where Purdy and the rest were smoking. She shook her head and said, "Oh my god," and the two of them walked away.

"See yous later," Pete shouted.

Sid passed them at the break, sparking a lighter with a cigarette behind an ear. He gave Nicky a nod.

"Is that the sicko?" Pete said. "What's he doing giving you the nod?

"I dunno."

"Bloody moshers. Look at the state of them."

"They don't bother anyone."

"I wouldn't mind bothering the Nazi Witch though – as long as she kept the big dirty boots on."

Nicky shook his head. "You need castrated."

They headed for the fence. Somewhere someone yelled: "YOU. WAIT THE FUCK THERE." They carried on.

"FUCK-ING WAIT," the voice went.

It was for them. They stopped. Purdy had been leaning on the fence, waiting. Now he was coming fast across the playground.

"Awright, Purdy," Pete called back.

Nicky tugged his sleeve. Pete shook him off.

Purdy stopped. He pointed into Pete's face. "You're a wee dick."

"What?"

"Quit smiling. Fuckin' Skelf. You're a wee dick. I know what you fuckin' said." He stepped closer and glared, white fat folding under his chin.

"I didn't say anything."

15

"Fuck off. Jennifer Black told me."

"I dunno what you're going on about."

Purdy pointed at Nicky. "You heard it. You wee poofs are always together."

Nicky looked away.

"Pie supper face, she said."

Pete held his hands up, shaking his head.

"Fuckin' pie supper?"

Purdy reached and grabbed the neck of Pete's jacket. He pushed till Pete's legs buckled. Folk came running from different corners. Pete was flattened, turning dark red. Blood spotted his hands and he waved them about, as if he was afraid of staining Purdy's jacket. Purdy knelt on his stomach, pulled out a chubby marker and bit the lid off. He grabbed Pete's throat. In slow letters he wrote PIE across his forehead. He went back over it, making the word bolder, putting a full stop.

PIE.

He spat the lid into Pete's face, clicked it on the pen and got to his feet.

"You're the fuckin' pie now."

Purdy laughed. He zipped the marker in his pocket and went off. Pete rolled onto his side, the ink shining. Nicky took a step, but Pete scrambled up and walked off, pushing past everyone with his head hanging, wiping the word with the back of his hand.

"What's that all about?" It was Sid, standing next to him.

"Nothing. He just said something stupid."

They watched Pete jog round the corner.

"Poor guy," Sid said. "Pretty funny though. Pie."

The bell rang.

"You still coming later?"

"What?"

"To mine, for a jam."

"Not sure if I'll make it."

"Just come."

The playground was emptying out. Nicky glanced at his watch. There'd been a chemical smell off the marker, as if the ink was permanent. He looked towards the toilets, where Pete'd be locked in a cubicle if any of them still had locks. There were no mirrors in there either.

Nicky went towards the main entrance and sunk in with the crowd and squeezed through the doors.

Everyone was gone, except for a wee kid on crutches waiting for a taxi. Pete wasn't at the gates. Nicky crossed the road to the phone box, called home and left a message. He hung up, then unscrunched the piece of paper from his pocket.

No one answered the doorbell. Up at Sid's bit, the houses were huge and white and someone had once bought a pair that backed on to each other, torn one down and replaced it with a tennis court. He waited then pressed the button again. When no one answered, he tried the door handle. It clicked open, leaking out a faint buzz of guitar. He kept hold of the handle, staring at the set of keys hanging from the other side. There was a thick cream carpet between him and the stairs. He went to undo his laces then stopped, wiped his feet and walked across. The banister creaked under his hand. It was carved wide and smooth and dotted with brass studs to prevent you sliding down on your arse. At the top he chose the door covered in yellow POLICE INCIDENT DO NOT CROSS tape. He nudged it open.

"Why don't you just wear the fuckin' specs," Sid shouted.

The bass player stood close, squinting and trying to copy his fingers.

Sid let go of the guitar. "Get a strap that holds them on your head."

"I don't need the fuckin' specs."

"You're always a beat behind man. And plus it's only four notes. Just fuckin' memorise it."

"Piss off, man," the other boy said. He flicked the hair out his face and noticed Nicky standing there. "Is that the guy?"

"Yeah."

"From the church?"

Sid said, "This is Fadge."

The boy with the bass nodded.

"Sticks are on the kit." Sid started playing again.

Fadge's eyes followed Nicky across the room. Sid smacked his shoulder.

"I'm trying to teach you this fuckin' thing."

Nicky sat on the stool and pulled the drums in tighter. He turned a screw on a stand and lowered it.

"It's CIV," Sid asked him, "D'you know CIV?"

Fadge said, "No one fuckin' does. What's the point even doing it?"

"Cos it's a great song. And the bassline's simple enough even for a fanny like you." Sid came over and skimmed a finger across a cymbal edge. "You should just do whatever drummers do. Try and keep up. After four." He walked back to the mike. "FOUR."

Guessing where the kick and snare beats should go was easy. Sid yelled for him to play the toms and he filled the spaces in-between. Fadge quit eyeing him and concentrated on his bass, mouth hanging open and tongue sliding at his bottom lip. A chord blared and Sid sang, foot stamping the base of the mike stand. It was built from an upside down flowerpot, a broom handle shoved in the hole and brown tape round the mike at the top. Nicky watched, matching the beat.

Sid screamed: "CYMBALS."

Nicky switched to the cymbal and hit until his arms ached. A skeleton face was grinning from a poster, black gaps between the teeth and its eyeballs rolled right back. Fadge was hunched over the bass, a bit of spit dribbling out. Sid screwed his eyes and meant the words, the guitar hanging at his crotch.

Fadge quit, then Sid, then Nicky. Sweat trickled into his shirt. They looked at Fadge. One string lay slack across the bass.

"Snapped it." He tugged it free, wiped his mouth on his sleeve and went, "Fag?"

They slumped on a worn-out couch, feet on the edge of a glass table covered in used plates and glasses. Crumbs were scattered about and unboxed CDs stacked in a silver tower.

"D'you think his clothes are a bit shite?" Sid said.

Nicky was behind the drums. He looked at himself. "It's my uniform."

"I mean the gear you had on the other day."

"That's Sunday stuff."

"S'pose you'll be at the back, so no one'll see."

"Who gives a shit about the drummer anyway?" Fadge said.

"Your wee sister."

Fadge threw a lighter and it bounced of the side of Sid's head. He blew smoke at the ceiling.

"Open a window," Sid said.

"Fuck off you."

"You're the fat prick smoking."

"You're the one about to spark up."

"It's my room but."

Neither of them moved. Three tall windows looked out at the street behind them. Balled-up clothes were stuffed under the bed and spilling from a line of wardrobes. Fadge and Sid sat watching themselves in the mirrored doors.

Nicky nodded at the stereo. "Does that record player work?"

"My old boy gave me that, plus all his God-awful ancient records – Bob Dylan and Leonard Cohen and all the other moany old bastards. It's fucked anyway." He picked up a remote, aimed it at the CD player.

"Not this old shite again."

"Fadge son, this is the Ramones. You need to show some decorum."

Fadge frowned.

"Fadge'd rather be listening to Ocean Colour Scene."

"Shut it. I had like one CD. And it was a present.

This stuff all sounds the same, man. The same three pish notes over and over."

Sid pushed the earring through his ear and laughed. "What?"

"Nothing."

They smoked and listened to the music. Felt pen graffiti covered the white walls. Different handwriting. I DID SID AND HAD HIS KIDS, then underneath I DID SID I GOT AIDS. Sid tapped some ash and rested the cigarette in the ashtray.

"Here. This is for you." He stood, pulled a cassette from a pocket and stretched across the drums. Nicky took it and turned it over in his hands. SID'S GREATEST SHITS it said, then a skull and crossbones.

He fell back on the couch. "So Mondays are cool?"

"Mondays?"

"For practise. We'll be playing the scout hall soon."

Fadge sighed. "The scout hall again. For fuck's sake."

"When are you sorting us out a gig? Lazy big bastard."

"Monday's fine," Nicky said.

"Good." Sid crushed the cigarette end. "So you're a Fuck Trumpet now."

"What?"

"Welcome to the Fuck Trumpets." He spread his arms out.

"Next week you get your tattoo," Fadge said.

Pammy

Sach sat by himself on the wheelchair ramp. His toes pointed together, a black school bag between his knees. It was covered in Tippex. He raised his eyebrows and went back to staring across the playground. Nicky gave the Tippex a read, then nudged the bag with a toe.

"D'you like all those bands?"

Sach shrugged, bowl-cut flopping in his eyes. Nicky sat next to him on the ramp and they gazed across at the fence, watching the mob chuck stones at each other.

Nicky looked at the bag again. "Slayer. Are they any good?"

"Affirmative."

"What about The Cure?"

"Miserable bastards. It's my brother's old bag."

"I'm in a band now."

"What's your instrument?"

"Drums."

Sach tutted. "Shit. I've been seeking a drummer since time began. What's your combo called?"

"Fuck Trumpets."

"What?"

"Fuck Trumpets."

Sach rubbed his chin. "Good name. Think I've

heard of yous. You won't be allowed in the papers. The DJs'll have to call you Eff Star Star Star Trumpets."

"What's your band called?"

"Princess Diana's Backstreet Abortion."

"That's worse."

"Mibbe."

The bell went and they slung their bags on and trudged towards the entrance. "Where's Pete?" Sach said. "Heard he had to go to hospital. After yesterday."

"It was just a bit of pen."

"I hate Purdy. Wish I could pen him."

"What'd you write?"

"I am a fat waste of skin. Please exterminate me."

Nicky laughed. "Teachers keep loading me up with Pete's homework. As if I'm his nurse or something."

"Is he mad at you? Cos you didn't jump in?"

"Would you have jumped in on Purdy?"

Sach shrugged.

He left the sheets lying in the porch, went down the steps and stopped on the path. There was a chance someone would trample them or kick them under the doormat. If Pete didn't get them, he'd get the blame.

The curtains were drawn tight and the room flashed with colours from the TV. Pete didn't say anything when Nicky knocked, or when he snuck his head round the door. The room stank. When he asked if he was feeling better, Pete swore and chucked the playstation controller on the floor.

"Is that new?"

Next to his bed a massive poster of Pammy stretched to the ceiling. They both gazed at her. The top half of her tits bulged out the swimsuit, which made a red V between her legs. She half-smiled, teasing because this was the closest you'd ever get to her, her lips fat and pink and her hair golden and tangled from rolling around in the sand. It hung over one eye. The other followed you around the room, icy blue and lined with black.

"I've got homework for you."

It was too dim to see any black smudges left on Pete's forehead.

"Just leave it there."

"Sorry. They made me take it."

"Just leave it."

"Coming in tomorrow?"

Pete reached for the controller. "Mibbe."

Nicky left the sheets on the desk and started flicking through an old *Loaded*.

"So is that it?"

"Yeah."

"See you later then."

Nicky nodded, took one last look at Pammy and left.

At the play park, older folk smoked by the swings and tried to set the bin on fire. The football pitch next to it used to be ash, before they turned it to grass and fenced it up.

Years ago, Pete and him would ride the bikes across it, practising skids and covering each other in red dust. Some kids used to do the ghostie. You cycled fast between the goals and at the last moment grabbed the cross bar, hanging while the bike kept going then crashed in the mud. Nicky tried it once, when Pete dared him and some girls were watching from the side. He'd cycled fast, stood on the pedals but wasn't tall enough. His fingertips caught the goals, knees knocked the handlebars and the bike collapsed. He landed smack on top. Blood blobbed out where the cog bit into his leg and he covered his face, arm jammed between his teeth. Pete got him to his feet and limped him home, and he sobbed the whole way. Later on, the bike appeared, leaning against his house.

The folk were crowded round the bin now, flames licking up and sending out black smoke. One of the boys stood by the swings, trying to smash a bottle on the red spongy floor. He flung it hard but it just bounced.

Nicky turned back the way he'd come. He had headphones in, the yellow walkman playing Sid's tape. The song was called "White Riot". He tried to walk in time with the drums but quickly ran out of breath.

Clarence

Pete was up ahead. He was with Danny Donnelly. First years parted to let Danny Donnelly past, squashing against hedges on one side and parked cars on the other. His bag hung off one shoulder, a cap stuck far back on his head. Folk said he punched a teacher once – Fat Jacques the French teacher. Fat Jacques didn't do anything about it because of Danny Donnelly's family.

Nicky was alone behind the sixth year girls, watching the legs work, the heels press into the pavement and the muscles swell in the shiny material. Soon half a stiffy snuck up. He pulled his jacket down, put his hand in a pocket and folded it.

They had seats next to each other in registration. Nicky climbed on his stool and said morning and Pete nodded, staring ahead at the blackboard. Behind them a boy whispered, "Awright Skelf. How's the head?"

The teacher came in and took his seat behind the desk. His head was shrunk into his shoulders. He was so pale he could be dead, hair plastered back and long sharp nose like a blade stuck from his face. He was ancient. Pete said he'd been there when his uncle was at school. He said it was his uncle that came up with the nickname – the Count.

"Show us your forehead," the boy behind said.

The count croaked through the register. When he called Pete's name the boy coughed into his hand.

"PIE."

Folk laughed and Pete's eyes fell on the desk.

He bunched his fists inside his sleeves. A long line of traffic sprayed by, the stripes on his jacket reflecting off headlights. At the garage he stopped and clicked the yellow walkman off and tugged out the earphones.

The woman at the counter bleeped the things, dropping them in a carrier bag.

"That all?"

"Can I get twenty Mayfair too."

"What?"

"Cigarettes. Twenty Mayfair please."

"You sixteen?"

He nodded. She reached behind, fumbling for the packet and examining his face.

"Sure you're sixteen?"

"Yeah."

Once they were bleeped and in the bag she said, "Can't get any I.D for being sixteen anyway."

"And Rizlas please."

"What?"

"Some Rizla papers. The green ones."

"Cheers for getting this man," Sid said. He peeled the tab, tearing the plastic. "Want one?"

Nicky shook his head.

"You ever tried?"

"Does your mum not mind?"

"Been doing it since I was about nine."

"Nine?"

"And she smokes like a big chimney anyway." He laid two cigarette papers on the glass table. "I put this on for you."

"What?"

"The CD. Green Day."

"Thought they were rubbish."

"It's bubblegum shite obviously. But the early stuff's awright. When they went to the major label, they got really crap. Same thing that always happens, man. Sell outs."

The brown guts of a cigarette were emptied on the papers. Sid chose a video box from the shelf. It said *ARMY OF DARKNESS* across the front, a man in a torn shirt standing over the words and waving a chainsaw. The lid popped open and out came a wee block of hash. Lighter flicked on, Sid thumbed the flame high, heated the block till it charred and crumbled over the tobacco.

"Where's Fadge?" Nicky said.

"Grounded. He got pished here the other night then went home and spewed all over their new carpets. His mum went nuts. Phoned my mum, trying to get her to pay for it. Just cos her son's a fuckin' lightweight."

"What about practise?"

"She'll let him out of it. She always does." He went over and changed the CD then sat, twisting the papers into a point. A Hoover was going somewhere in the house. He sparked up. "Want some? It's only soap bar."

"I'm awright."

"Ever got high before?"

Nicky shrugged.

"I'm shit at rolling man. Wait till you meet our mate the Wizard. He was doing engineering at uni but says he dropped out to build joints instead."

"I know this song. It's off the tape."

"Yup – Rancid. One of the greatest albums ever made."

Sid pushed the earring around in its hole, letting smoke steam from his mouth. The bass solo started. They listened. Sid closed his eyes and smiled.

When it finished, Nicky said, "Can Fadge play like that?"

"You joking? He only knows how to use one string, man. Check his bass next practise – the low one's pure manky. Brown, like fuckin' rust and the other three are brand new."

Nicky smiled and relaxed into the couch. He let his head roll back against the cushion and his eyes swirl round the pattern of flowers plastered In the middle of the ceiling.

"By the way," Sid said, "don't worry about him. Fadge, I mean. He doesn't know shit about shit. It's my band. I get to have in it who I like. And plus, it was him that made me give Shanks the boot in the first place."

"The last guy?"

"Yeah. Shanks. The silly prick. Him and Fadge's wee sister."

"What happened?"

Sid waved the question away.

The Rancid CD played. Sid worked his way through the joint, dipping his free hand into the crisps Nicky had brought, shovelling them into his mouth and crunching with his mouth open. Out in the hall the Hoover hummed passed the door. The skeleton face stared from the poster, its nose an empty black splodge.

Soon Sid's eyes were closed, his jaws still working and Rancid were singing about a Cadillac. Nicky picked CDs from the tower and leafed through: DESCENDENTS; THE MR T. EXPERIENCE; BLACK FLAG; BAD RELIGION. The backs of the discs were scratched to bits. At the door the Hoover droned and droned. Back and forward. Bumping the door open a crack. It started choking – clanging as if something metal was stuck in its mouth and went silent.

"Clarence."

Nicky put the CDs back. A woman had shouted it. There was a pause then she called again, right through the door.

"CLARENCE."

Sid's eyes popped open. He jumped up. He crossed the room, shaking his head and muttering, "Fuck off. Fuck off."

When he came back Nicky was waiting with his jacket on.

"I'd better go."

Sid went in his pocket and brought out a handful of coins and crumpled notes. "Here, for the stuff." He took the CD out the stereo and put it in its box. "Take this too. It's a classic so be careful. Put it on a tape or something. You coming to the scout hall?"

Nicky shrugged.

"The scout hall on Saturday. See some shite bands and meet everyone. Come." He reached and tapped Nicky's shoulder, then stared at his feet, toes wriggling in his socks.

When he was outside Nicky counted the money and shoved it in his pocket. It was far too much.

She'd been coming out the house when he reached the end of the path.

"I knew it was you," she said, "from the stripes on your jacket. How come you're here?" She stood close, but didn't move for a hug.

"Just passing."

She was going to meet someone, so he said he'd go with her to the bus stop. They walked the spiral from Ruth's street without speaking. Before they turned on to the main road she stopped, feet together and stared at her boots.

"What do you think of these? Be honest."

"I like them."

"D'you mean in a pervy way or do you actually like them?"

"I just mean I like them."

"You're staring."

"Cos you asked."

"Do I look like a hooker?"

"They're nice."

"Quit staring." Ruth sighed and walked on. "I had this other pair a few years ago. Mum wouldn't let me wear them to church. My dad let me get them, then the two of them had a massive fall out. They laced right up the front. I loved them, but now I see pictures of them and it's like yuck. They were hooker boots."

Nicky shrugged. "I've never seen a hooker."

Her heels clicked on the pavement. Up ahead the bus stop was empty. They went under a lamppost, the light flickering and Nicky pointed.

"My mum used to make me come in when the streetlights came on. When I was a wee guy."

"Right."

"My friend Pete got to stay out later with his big brother. I got pure jealous."

She didn't reply.

"Shame the two of us weren't wee pals back then," he said.

"You were always ignoring me." She peered up the road.

"I was shy. You were a girl."

"Still am."

When they arrived under the bus shelter she said, "You don't have to wait."

"Got nothing else to do."

"Phone me next time. Instead of just turning up. I feel bad."

"I was just passing by." A bus appeared and he stuck his arm out.

"I'll see you later," Ruth came close, then backed away. "You stink of smoke."

The bald driver gave her her ticket with a big grin. He watched in his mirror as she strode down the aisle and the doors hissed and clapped shut. The bus pulled away and Nicky sat on the metal bench, rubbing his shins. He'd walked fast and Ruth didn't live anywhere near Sid's. He sniffed his jacket.

There was a way to talk to girls. He'd seen Pete do it. Pete would start conversations with them, the best-looking ones and keep it going, never caring if he looked like a dick. They laughed at him, even when they were older and his jokes were pathetic. Pete was fearless.

When he was in second year Nicky tried to tell a girl a joke – what does DNA stand for? National Dyslexic Association. She walked away without laughing. Later he saw her on the couch, a friend on each side shaking their heads. The girl was covering her face, shuddering. He'd been in her class since primary, just forgot she was dyslexic. They were all in her house – he could remember the smell of cooking in the place. It was her party. Thinking of it made his stomach hollow.

When he reached his house, he sniffed the jacket again. He turned and went once more round the block.

Mack

He got close and mumbled, but they didn't move. He spoke up. There was a tree at the edge of the pavement, roots bursting through the concrete and narrowing the street. It was the stupidest moment to try and pass. Making himself as thin as he could, he tried to slip in-between. His bag nudged the blonde girl into a hedge. The other one staggered over a root.

"What the hell," she shouted. "Wee freak."

He caught up. Pete took a glance. Danny Donnelly's eyes stayed fixed ahead, puffed with sleep. He smoked quickly, scratching the side of his head where the hair was shaved right in.

After a while Pete said, "Done anything for this physics test?"

"Fuck all." Danny Donnachie's voice was low and you had to strain to hear.

"It's a lot of shite. My brother told me Old Rubberfud got caught wanking under a desk once."

Danny Donnelly smoked.

"You seen how he's always putting his hands on Nick's shoulders," Pete said, "giving him massages while he recites all the equations?"

"Get lost," Nicky said.

"He calls you his boy wonder."

Danny Donnelly pinged his fag end at the pavement.

"Fuckin' boy wonder." Pete said.

One of Danny Donnelly's hands had gone yellow, someone said, from smoking. He rubbed an eye and yawned.

"Doing anything at the weekend?" Pete asked him.

Danny Donnelly finished his yawn and clamped his teeth. "Dunno. Probably get a bevvy."

"Yeah. Same."

"How you getting it?"

"Get my brother to go in."

Danny Donnelly looked at him. "Get him to get mine then, eh?"

"Yeah. I can ask him."

"Will he but?"

Pete shrugged. "He's cool."

"Voddy. I need a full bottle. Pay you after."

Pete turned to Nicky. "Suppose you'll be busy on Sunday, Bible-bashing."

Danny Donnelly scratched his head again, where moles were dotted on the scalp.

Mack stared at the mound of cream, dragged it around the mug and sank it with his spoon. Back at the church a kid had taken a hockey stick to a door, smashing a spider web on the glass panel.

"Lots of folk tonight," Nicky said.

Mack nodded. "Not enough fifty pences to cover the damage though."

"You should make it more to get in."

"We discussed that. It'll discourage them from coming."

"Then you won't have to worry about them smashing the place up."

Mack half-smiled and shook his head. "They need a place. And we need to witness. To be honest, bud, we might not be running next year anyway. There's not enough of us. I can't do it alone."

He pushed the hair off his forehead and took a drink. There was a black and white photo behind him – Eric Clapton strumming a guitar in his beard and glasses, eyes shut and chin collapsing into his neck. Mack leaned back and his head knocked the frame.

"What would you do if it wasn't on?"

Nicky shrugged.

"You're there most Fridays. What if you joined the team? You've got your head screwed on. Maybe some of them would relate to you. What d'you reckon?"

Nicky put the mug to his lips. The coffee machine at the counter went off, hissing and spluttering and Mack stared over the table, eyebrows raised.

When it shut up, he said, "Come on bud. You'll be there anyway. We'd just need you a bit earlier to help set up, then stay on to get the church back in order. You did that tonight anyway."

"Some of them are older than me. Bigger anyway."

"Doesn't matter. And none of us have been hit." Mack grinned. "Yet."

Nicky turned the mug on its saucer. A group of girls from the year below sat silently at the next table, all dolled up, empty mugs pushed in the middle. One of them kept glancing over.

"By the way," Mack said, "did you get baptised when you were wee?"

Nicky frowned at the girl and she blinked away. "I don't think so."

"So that's another thing we'll need to start thinking about. Baptism."

"Before I can be a leader?"

"No – cos it's what we're meant to do."

Nicky nodded. He spooned the cream from the mug and dumped it on the saucer.

Scout Hall

He folded the paper and jammed it in. The letterbox was too wee. He barged with an elbow and forced it until it fell, flapped open in the porch. The front headline was shredded, bold black letters saying: *Repainted Bays Bring Parking Woe*. It didn't matter. No one would complain. At the next house last week's issue was kicked in the corner.

There was a boy who'd had the round before Nicky. For months he'd been dumping papers and collecting his pay and no one noticed. He only got fired when someone found a bundle floating in the river, caught up in rocks and turning to papier mâché. He'd hidden a load under his bed and under a stack of coal at the bottom of his garden and dug holes and buried them in the woods at the edge of the pitches. He said he was glad he got caught. All he could think about was dumping the papers. Couldn't even sleep. Every week he got landed with more. He was planning on a massive bonfire somewhere but couldn't work out where, didn't know how he'd get all the copies there. He said he'd been off school for weeks and was about to have a nervous breakdown and had quit caring about the money. He'd stopped spending it.

Nicky got to Pete's house. The gate squeaked and he squinted at Pete's bedroom window. All he could see was Pammy's elbow and a stripe of red. He went to ring the doorbell but stopped, bent and lifted the doormat and slipped the paper under the corner. When he reached his own house he was done.

He threw the bright orange bag under the stairs and opened the loft. Cymbals rang softly as he dragged the old sheet off the drum kit. The yellow walkman was in his pocket. During the round he'd been listening to Sid's tape, in his mind practising the beat from the Rancid song, drumming on his thighs when no one was around. He sat, earphones in and pressed play. A few seconds in, cramp seized his legs. He rewound and tried again.

Three boys in black T-shirts were smoking by the door, passing round a plastic bottle with the label torn off. Stones crunched under Nicky's feet. One of them coughed and the bottle disappeared behind their legs.

"Relax," the middle one said. "It's just some wee guy."

The corridor walls were stuck with pictures of scouts. They wore kilts and neck scarfs, hands behind backs for troop photos or out in a field somewhere, crouched over frying pans. At the end of the corridor a man waited behind a school desk.

"Hi Nicky," he said, "How are you?"

"Fine."

"I didn't know you came to these things." He made a mark on his sheet of paper.

"Do I just go in?"

"Once you've paid your quid."

Nicky fished out the money and dropped it in the

ice cream tub. The man took a rubber stamp and put a red smudge on his hand.

"Say hi to your mum for me."

The double doors swung open and two girls came out, one in a Descendents T-shirt. He edged against the wall, smiling and knocked off a blue-tacked poster. It flapped to the ground. The girls passed, ignoring him and he caught hold of the door and went in.

A three-piece band was on the stage, lit up by fluorescent yellow light. Out in the hall it was too dim to see anyone. The guitar player's face was painted white with black circles round his eyes and black lipstick. He was doing a solo, his fingers crawling up the neck but all you could hear was the drums. Behind them a broom stood against the wall next to some stacked buckets. Nicky searched for an empty space. Everyone was clustered in groups, staring. He faced the band, unzipped his jacket. The heating was up too high.

Someone jabbed him in the ribs. Sid. He grabbed Nicky's hood and dragged him off to the back corner where Fadge was sitting on a tower of plastic chairs like a tennis umpire. He nodded.

Sid put his mouth to Nicky's ear. "This is fake goth shite. They're called Chaos Engine." He nudged Nicky's ribs and laughed.

The song finished and Fadge cupped both hands round his mouth. "SHEEEEEEIIIIITE."

"Fuck off," the singer said into the mike. He tried to get his guitar tuned but the drums began again. Sid groaned and another boy, slumped against the chairs mimed a cigarette.

They walked round to a wee set of steps stuck on the side of the building. Fadge and Sid sat. Nicky stood opposite next to the other boy. Fadge got his fag going and said, "This is pure shite. Where is everyone?"

"No one could get a drink."

"This is Glove by the way," Sid said.

The other boy waved at Nicky. He was wearing black nail polish.

"And Glove," Sid said, "meet the Messiah."

"What?" Nicky said.

"We decided. You're the Messiah. Sent from above to save the Fuck Trumpets."

"From that bastard Shanks." Fadge said.

"Fadge – when'll you and Shanks quit acting like daft lassies?"

"Fuck off Glove. It's Shanks's fault. When'll he quit acting like a massive prick?"

Glove rolled his eyes and sat on the step in front. "You even asked your sister about it?"

"I don't even want to talk to that wee cow."

Sid sighed. "Boys. I'm so bored of this shite."

"He should quit standing up for Shanks but," Fadge said. "He'll never let you shag him Glove."

"You might though."

"Fuck off."

"Glove is a wee gay boy," Sid told Nicky.

"I'm not," Glove took a draw. "Not totally."

"How gay then?"

"Gayer than you, but not as gay as Fadge. He's so gay he can't even admit it to himself."

"Fuck off."

Glove tapped his balls. "Got a homo-ing device,"

"What about the Messiah then?" Fadge said.

"I dunno yet. He's hardly even spoke."

They all looked at Nicky.

"I'm not."

Sid laughed. "Never stopped Glove before."

"Better watch yourself," Fadge said.

They smoked the rest of their fags. When Fadge was done he mashed his into the wall. "Christ. I need a drink."

The other two nodded.

"Bring me some water then." Nicky said.

"What?"

"If you bring me some water, I can try turning it into wine. Since you asked."

Fadge and Sid stared.

Glove gave him a wee grin. "He means like Jesus. Morons. The Messiah."

"I know," Fadge said. "But it's a pish joke."

There was a splat. Egg dripped down the wall next to them. Another exploded, closer.

"Shit," Glove said. He shoved Nicky up the steps. "Duck."

Fadge hunched, hugging his knees. "Fuckin' hell. I thought they'd quit this shite."

Bits of shell sprayed over their huddle. Feet scuffed up the lane and more eggs thudded against the hall.

"Who is it?" Nicky said.

"Pricks from your school."

Sid lobbed a stone in the air like a grenade.

"FUCKIN' MOSHERS," someone yelled. Shadows turned out the lane, under the streetlights. Most of them had caps on, long cartons of eggs open in their hands.

"Make a bolt," Sid said, "Slack Grannies'll be on any minute." He pulled his jacket over his face and ran. The rest followed. Splatters hit one of Nicky's trainers. Two wee guys were surrounded at the gate, egged point blank.

On the way down the corridor, Glove elbowed Nicky. "It's just a laugh. I'm not actually gay. Not really."

"This is proper old school shit," Sid told him.

Slack Grannies were on stage uncoiling guitar leads and fiddling with amplifiers. The drummer tweaked his snare and took his t-shirt off. The bass player used to be at their school – Pete called him Dead Cat Boy. An anarchy sign was felt-tipped on the singer's white vest. He unclipped the microphone and wrapped the wire around his hand, picked up the stand and launched it like a spear at the stacked buckets. The drummer clicked his sticks.

They played fast. The girl with the guitar faced her amplifier and rolled the volume up. Hair fell over the drummers face, plastered down with sweat. A cigarette poked out. He bit it in one corner, puffing breaths out the other side and flung his arms around. There was a concrete block in front of his kick drum, stopping it getting away.

The boys started shoving into each other. Nicky went to step away but Sid grabbed him and pushed him into Glove. Glove put an arm round his should-er, spinning him and Fadge came from behind and shoved him into the edge of the stage. He looked up, winded. Dead Cat Boy grinned, reached out a boot and nudged him back. More folk had piled in. A chain from someone's jeans whipped his leg and damp hair lashed his face. It went in his mouth. Sweat from other bodies smeared his jacket. Something cold closed round his wrist and tugged, yanking his arm until he was free and safe. He looked, gasping. It was the girl in the Descendents t-shirt.

"You're too wee," she said in his ear. "You'll get fuckin' killed."

He smiled and tried to say thanks but his breath was gone. She'd turned back to watch.

Straight Edge

Ruth blew in her hands. "Freezing in here."

"What'd you do last night?"

"Babysitting. Again. I called to see if you'd come over." She reached and pressed the red smudge on his hand. "What's that?"

"From the scout hall. I went to see some bands."

She picked one of her fingernails. "Last night?"

He nodded.

"D'you not wash?"

Mack walked in and waited in front of semi-circle of chairs. The talking faded. He clapped his hands together and welcomed everyone, apologised for the broken heating. He said they were going to warm up with some old Sunday school songs. "In these Arctic conditions the actions are mandatory," he said. Everyone bowed heads for the opening prayer.

Someone strummed the chords on an old acoustic guitar. The words came from a Bible verse: *The name of the Lord is a strong tower. The righteous run into it and they are saved.* At "strong" Mack made you flex your biceps. At "run" you had to jog on the spot.

They sat. An older girl got up and showed some slides of wee kids in Africa. Most of them had AIDS, she said, and she'd gone there to help build a new school. She paused every few sentences, reached and pushed her glasses up her face. Her face was flat with only a thin wedge of nose. In her slides the building was just a shadowy box of bricks, messy lines of cement in-between and carpeted with sand. All the black kids were laughing, delighted. There was a photo of them ganged round the girl, hugging her legs and fingers holding the peace sign, while she beamed at the camera. Her nasally voice stopped and she admired the picture glowing on the wall, her face making a sad match.

A new boy got up to read the Bible passage. It was the parable of the sower: a farmer scatters his seeds. Some falls in the path and birds eat it. Some falls on shallow soil, grows fast and burns in the sun. Some falls in thorns and gets choked to death. A wee bit lands in good soil, and it grows and grows and grows. New boy was nervous and stuttered his way through, tracing the words with a finger. "Whoever has ears, let them hear," he read and closed his bible.

"Amen." Mack took the floor. "Whoever has ears, let them hear," he repeated and for a moment he went silent.

When he opened his eyes, he switched on the overhead projector. He slid on a picture of a man dressed as a scarecrow with a daft grin, fake nose and straw hair hanging round his manky face.

"This is Worzel Gummidge," Mack said, "the greatest scarecrow that ever lived."

Folk laughed.

Mack told them how the scarecrow came to life, how he would switch between different heads when he required certain skills. He was petrified of bonfires. If ever he was scared or cornered he froze, becoming a lifeless scarecrow again.

Mack paused and swallowed. "Jesus' parable of the sower speaks to everyone. None of you," he waved a finger around the hall, "or me are safe from this simple wee tale. Especially not old Worzel." He smiled and slid the picture off. The next slide said **1. The Seed on the Path**, three bullet points underneath.

Nicky shifted his leg till it grazed Ruth's. Hers inched away and she cleared her throat. He stared at the carpet. If you stared long enough the pattern became evil wee faces. Once they appeared, he let his eyes cross and the faces blurred and rose, swarming around. He moved his foot, squashing them back into the floor.

He blinked and looked and Mack had turned to their side of the group.

"So many of us," he was saying, "Are like Worzel. We have different heads for different situations. And like the seeds on the path, we've never even sprouted the tiniest of roots."

Bible spread in one hand, he turned to the other side of the hall. Nicky dipped his head again. He rubbed his thumbs across his palms, feeling wee bubbles of skin. The drumsticks were giving him blisters. It'd never happened before. Janet Johnson had glared over her piano that morning and when the service ended she took him aside and told him to never play like that again. It'd been so fast people couldn't fit in the words. If he wanted to be a real musician he had to learn to listen. She pointed at her ears.

Sid wanted to play much faster – as fast as Slack Grannies. He said so after the gig. He said Slack Grannies rehearsed four times a week. When they'd finished school, none of them took proper jobs. The band was their job. Soon they'd be in a recording studio, making their demo CD. Record labels were waiting to hear it. The singer was called Gerry. "Gerry doesn't give a flying fuck though man," Sid said. "He says the labels don't know shit. They're full of corporate gobshites in Paul Smith suits." Gerry had a massive black hammer and sickle tattoo on his chest and he smoked skinny wee joints without tobacco, just pure weed. They looked like stick insects with the legs pulled off, Sid said.

The wee hall was silent. Mack coughed. He took the slide off and pushed a second one on. **2. The Shallow Ground** it said. Three more bullet points were underneath.

Ruth yawned and blew into her hands again. She

tapped Nicky and said, "D'you remember that scare-crow programme?"

"Kind of. Not really."

"It sounds freaky. I reckon everyone that made those old kids' programmes was on drugs, don't you?"

He smiled. She crossed her legs and her shin rested against him.

She said, "I never knew Mack was so mental when he was younger. The other night he was telling me all his stories. Well, some of them. I'm sure there's loads. D'you know his friend ended up in prison? He was in a fight outside a pub and punched this guy and the guy fell, smacked his head on the kerb and died."

Nicky glanced. Mack was talking to the new boy in the corner, shaking his hand.

Ruth went on, "So when this mate of his was in prison he ran out of cigarette papers and started using the Gideon bible. He was smoking the bible. Then one day he was in the middle of making it and the words caught his eye. So he shakes the stuff off the page and reads it. It was out the Gospels and he got converted."

"So d'you think he smoked the whole Old Testament?"

She frowned.

"Before he got to the Gospels I mean."

She tutted and shook her head. "Anyway, point is he gets out of prison and ends up convincing Mack to become a Christian."

Mack was packing his things into a rucksack. He looked over and both of them were staring. He grinned.

Ruth went back to picking her nail polish. "I want chips now. A big greasy bag of chips."

"Let's get chips then."

Her hands dropped to her sides. "It's too late. And I'll get fat."

"Come on," Nicky punched her arm softly. "Let's get some. The shop's still open and you're too skinny anyway."

"Should we? I can't stop thinking about them now." She leaned forward and grabbed his arm with both hands, "Where'll we go?"

"Anywhere you want."

She let go and jumped up. "I'll ask Mack. He can drive us."

The blonde girl was on her own in a skirt to her knees with a wee slit up the back. It looked too narrow to walk in. She was swivelling her arse and taking tiny steps like a wind up toy. The seam was straining.

"Awright," he said when he caught up.

Neither of them replied.

"Good weekend?"

"Heard you were at that mosher thing on Saturday," Pete said. "When d'you join that freak show."

"I play drums with some of them."

"You're in a mosher band? That's the gayest thing I've heard. Where's your mosher chain?"

"It's a punk band."

Pete laughed.

At the school gates Jennifer Black came towards them and he asked Danny Donnelly for a fag.

"Get to fuck," he told him.

Nicky walked away. He found Sach on the wheel-chair ramp. They nodded at each other and he sat.

"I went to that scout hall thing at the weekend."

"See any decent combos?"

"Slack Grannies. Mostly old-school stuff."

Sach nodded. "My brother was in a band with that guy. The singer. They fell out cos it was meant to be straight edge."

"What d'you mean?"

"Anti-drugs and anti-booze. Minor Threat and Black Flag for example. The other guy kept turning up pished and stoned the whole time."

"So your brother never drinks or anything?"

"We're forbidden. All intoxicants are forbidden."

The bell went and they both got up from the ramp.

"You'll never drink either?" Nicky said.

"I'm not supposed to get my hair cut either."

Nicky looked at his bowl cut. "Mibbe you shouldn't've bothered."

"Ha ha, fuck off," Sach said. "Yours isn't much better."

The blisters on his hands had burst and he'd peeled the flaps of dead skin away. Underneath the red flesh stung and seeped and left wet dots on the drumsticks.

"The middle bit sounds shite," Sid said.

Fadge sighed. "The whole song's shite. I hated it the first time, now I never want to hear it again."

"Try learning it. Messiah only heard it about five minutes ago and he knows it."

"Course he fuckin' does."

"And when you getting that string fixed man? You're a joke."

"Get off my case, man."

Sid turned to Nicky. "It's still too slow but. We need to do it again."

Fadge went to moan. Sid nodded the speed he wanted and Nicky clicked it in.

During the chorus the bedroom door opened. A girl came in. It was the scout hall girl, the one in the Descendents T-shirt. On her way across the room, she reached and twisted a tuning peg on Fadge's bass. He aimed a kick at her and she danced away grinning and sat on the couch, boots on the edge of the glass table. She was small, with short black hair.

When they were done, Fadge said, "What d'you want?"

"That sounded a bit shit. No offence."

"It's your idiot brother's fault," Sid said. "He's an embarrassment to your family."

The girl nodded, "Yeah. My mum's taking him to get put down."

"Why the hell are you here?" Fadge said.

"I thought we should spend more time together."

"We're busy. Fuck off home."

"Mum says you need to come home now or your dead. You're still grounded and she says you were only supposed to be out an hour. And you're a fat bastard."

Fadge mumbled and unplugged his bass, leaving the lead buzzing on the carpet.

"Sid," the girl said. "I need booze for the party."

"Me too," Fadge said.

"It's me and Melissa. We need voddy."

"Wine. And you owe us for the last time anyway."

"Right. Hang on." Sid picked up a piece of paper and smoothed it on his knee. He turned to Nicky. "What about you?"

Fadge started laughing. "Shit. I just noticed – Annie, you and him have the exact same hair cut."

Sid laughed.

The girl glared at Nicky. She chucked an empty fag packet at Fadge. "Fuck off Gordon."

"My party on Saturday," Sid said. "You need a bevvy. Place your order." He held the paper and pencil like a waiter.

"I didn't know about it."

"You're coming though. What you having? Your Uncle Sid'll sort it."

"I'll be awright."

Sid was waiting. Fadge and Annie were too.

Nicky picked a splinter from one of the drumsticks. He stared at the snare drum and shrugged. "Cider?"

"Good choice sir. I'll bring you with the biggest and nastiest bottle on the menu."

Fadge grinned. "The Messiah's getting fucked up." He slung the bass over his shoulder.

"Wait up." Annie said. On her way past, she gave Sid a punch.

The door closed behind them. "Those McFadgens are a bunch of bastards," he said, rubbing his arm.

Careers

The corner of the page was folded over, **January 24th** printed at the top. He could've flipped to the actual date but started here instead. This was where he'd given up last time – he hadn't even made it out of January. Mack had told them they should make a New Year's resolution, that they should make one every New Year. He called it a chance for renewal. Now the year was almost done and soon Nicky would have to pledge the next.

It should've been easy – each reading was only a couple of pages. Mack had even given him the book to get him started. *The New Testament in One Year*. Inside the front page he'd written in curly biro: *Eat your Bread daily bud!*

Jesus' words were printed in red. On January 24th he was choosing his disciples, telling them, "Take no bag for the journey, or extra tunic or sandals or staff. The worker is worth his keep."

There was a wee thought at the end of the passage. God chooses ordinary people for his extraordinary works, it said. Nicky closed the book, shoved it under the bed and clicked off the lamp. He turned on his side, pulled the covers high and closed his eyes. For a while he lay like that, then rolled on his back. The numbers on the clock glowed red.

The TV clicked on and he quickly jabbed the mute button. He jumped through the channels. He knew the number fine, but if you scrolled it made it seem less obvious. He passed the weatherwoman, pointing at her map, spoiled with leaking black clouds but flashing her big white smiles anyway, her yellow hair combed and sprayed in place. Next a man and another woman appeared. She was blonde too and bollock naked, riding the man. He tugged at his pyjamas. The woman's hair hung, hiding her face while she tied the man's hands to the top of the bed. You could see her tits. She leaned back and rode and the camera zoomed behind, showing her arse swivelling then focussing on her hand. She was rummaging under the covers. He took his waistband down. She brought something out, raised it and rammed it through the man's chest. It was thin and sharp, and she wrenched it free and stabbed him again. Then again. She was frantic, hacking his neck, bursting his eyeball. Puncturing him all over. Blood spurted everywhere, bright red, spraying their bodies and the bedsheets. The man was screaming, a black hole for a mouth.

Nicky flicked back. The forecast was finished. He killed the TV and rolled on his side, lying in the dark with his fingers round the stiffy.

He grabbed hold of the pipe. The big iron radiator was painted a sick looking white and he only made it to six before the heat scorched and he had to let go. A flake of paint stuck into his skin. The door opened and Pete came out the office. On the register their names had always been next to each other – even when they moved up to secondary, no one had snuck in-between.

"How was it?"

"Lot of shite," Pete whispered. "Says I should do a business degree. Fuck off mate."

Nicky stood.

"Saw you and the cock tease were out for coffees the other day. Playing at being grown ups?"

"Are you following me about?" Nicky said.

"She's a right wee ride though. Any joy yet?"

"She's taller than you." He went to step past.

Pete's hair had been shaved at the sides. The front wouldn't gel flat like Danny Donnelly's, because of his cows lick. "You going to ask about becoming a priest?" he said.

"Shut up."

Pete grinned and walked off.

Behind the desk a man sat with his forehead resting on his arms. Nicky coughed. The man spoke to the floor, "Wait please. You'll be called when I'm ready."

He went back into the corridor, leaned against the wall. The door opened and the man's head appeared.

"Nicholas."

He sat across from Nicky, eyes red at the edges and the start of a beard on his face. After scribbling something on a form he said, "Okay Nicholas," He sighed, "are you fine?"

"Yeah."

"Good. Well. What we'll be doing today is taking a good look at your future. Excuse me one moment."

He reached, fumbled in a cracked leather bag and brought out a packet of pills. He popped two and palmed them in his mouth. "Got the cold. Bad time of year for it." He pushed his fist against his lips and swallowed them dry.

"Your report here is pretty good," the man said. "Good results. Good predictions for this year." He smiled. His face looked clammy and the place stank of smoke and stale booze.

Nicky nodded.

"So. Any ideas what you want to do with yourself? Looking at your classes and predicted grades, I can make a few suggestions. There's nothing you've thought about doing? No career you can imagine yourself in?"

"Dunno."

"Got a favourite subject?"

"I don't mind music."

"What d'you play?"

"Drums."

"So this is about how you're going to earn you're living. We all have to somehow. These are important decision. Anything more concrete?"

Nicky shrugged.

He forced open a stuck drawer and took out some glossy magazines, opened the top one where a corner was folded, spun it and pushed it over. He tapped a finger. "How about giving this a look. A good fit with your subjects."

It was a greyish finger. The white on the nail chewed away.

"It's a business degree, but it's pretty broad. Lots

of space to specialise." He folded the corner down again and closed the magazine. "Give it a good look." Leaning back, he clasped his hands on his head. "Any questions?"

Nicky shook his head. A round sweat patch stained each of the man's armpits.

"So let's just leave it there. The bell's about to go after all." He stacked the other magazines and filed them away. "I'm here most weeks, Nicholas, so if you need any more advice, that's my job." Wide grin.

There were still about eight minutes until the bell rang. Nicky left the office and walked along the corridor to wait in the toilets, the magazine rolled up in his hand.

"They're monsters, Nicky," Mack was saying, "but if we ban one of them the rest'll quit coming. Then what's the point?"

Nicky nodded out the window of Mack's black Golf.

Local kids had spent the night booting footballs at the church ceiling until one of the lighting tubes came loose and fell. It exploded on the floor and they all ran off, shards and white dust everywhere. Sick was discovered dripping down one of the toilets and starting to dry in.

The tidy up took ages. He had to do the mopping. Mack had wheeled the yellow bucket over and it bumped his leg and soapy water sloshed out, wetting his jeans. They didn't have to mop every week, Mack said, but would he mind? Afterwards each of the leaders dragged over a plastic chair and they sat in a circle praying. When the church doors were locked Friday night was almost done, but Mack had twirled his car keys round one finger and said, "Fancy seeing what Ruthy's up to, bud?"

He stared through the car window at her front door. The light in her bedroom had just gone off. The door opened and she walked over, hugging herself with her hood up.

"I suppose it's better than them terrorising folk on the streets," Mack said. "They're coming round too. Calming down a bit, I reckon."

"Probably."

When Ruth was near the car Mack said, "Be a gent."

"What?"

"Be a gentleman bud, jump in the back."

He got out. Ruth touched his arm and waited for him to lift the seat and climb in the back. She pushed it in place and slid in.

"You two are late," she said.

Mack said, "Sorry m'dear. The thugs were reeking havoc as usual. Even bringing in the big man there in the back didn't scare them."

"They all just need a good slap," Ruth said.

"When are you coming to give them it then?"

She tugged her hood off, flipped the visor and checked herself in the mirror.

"Where we going?" Nicky said.

"How about the dancing?"

Ruth folded the visor away. "Let's go to the beach."

"It's dark and freezing," Mack said, "Plus it's miles away. You're far too young to be out at this time anyway."

She tapped his thigh with her knuckles. "Don't be boring. They do the best chips there."

"She loves her chips," Nicky said.

Ruth turned and frowned at him and reached for the seatbelt. Her buckle clicked and the car started and drove off.

It was noisy in the back, the tyres spinning over the road and the engine loud. Nicky leaned forward. The Counting Crows CD played and Mack was telling some story about Friday nights growing up in England. Ruth laughed hard, bouncing her head off the headrest.

Nicky said, "Will the chippy not be shut?"

No one replied.

He sank back in the seat.

Party

Sid said, "You're fuckin' early."

An older boy was stretched on the bed reading a magazine. Beside him sat a tray with cigarette papers, a lighter and wee plastic bags knotted at the top. Nicky walked by and nodded. He sat on the old couch next to Sid. Sid had a beer can at his lips, pinging the ring pull in time with the CD. He scrunched the can and left it to topple and leak on the table.

"Shit. Introductions," he said and waved an arm. "This is the Wizard."

The boy on the bed tipped an invisible hat. His hair was shaved down to stubble and he wore glasses with thick black frames.

"And this is the Messiah."

Nicky nodded again.

Sid pointed at the bed. "Ask him his actual name."

The boy sighed and said, "You always do this when it's new folk."

"Just ask him."

Nicky asked. "What's your name?"

"Merlin."

"You're so full of bullshit," Sid said

Merlin held a palm towards the ceiling. "God's honest truth. My folks are mad hippies. They were I mean."

"Bollocks," Sid turned to Nicky. "No one knows for sure cos none of us were at school with him. He's pure ancient. "

"Why don't you bring your birth certificate in?" Nicky said.

"Mad bastards like him aren't born. He's the – what's the fuckin' word – the by-product of some experiment."

The Wizard smiled, lifted the tray on his lap and went to work. No one spoke until *Rudy Can't Fail* came on the stereo.

"This is the Clash," Nicky said.

Sid leaned and ruffled his hair. He took his hand away and stared at it. "Your head's all crunchy, man."

"It's just a bit of gel."

He wiped his hand on Nicky's jeans. "You got London Calling?"

"Got it out the library."

The Wizard laughed. "A punk with a library card."

"Merlin loves Jethro Tull and all that pish. He's a sad, sad old bastard."

"The Tull are quality. Plus, you weren't calling me an old bastard when you needed the booze."

"Is that almost done?" Sid said.

He held up a long lumpy cone.

Nicky said, "That's a beast."

"This is what you call a beast." Sid heaved a carrier bag from the side of the couch and dumped it between them. Nicky stared and ran his hand across it. He slid the bag off and the bottle of cider lay there, fat and wet with condensation.

"Did you know that shit's made out of onions?"

"How d'you even know, Merlin? You don't even drink. Just sit there and smoke till you go blind. Or get so para you fling yourself out the window."

"Get to France, sir. That doesn't happen any more. Anyway, the weed's better for you. It's herbal. A gift from the earth."

"So are onions," Sid said.

"How much was it?" Nicky said.

"Don't worry son. It's your award. Best newcomer."

Nicky unscrewed the lid. He took a sniff and coughed.

"Onions," the Wizard said.

The doorbell rang. Sid left the room. Nicky sat for a while, hearing the front door open and close, downstairs filling with voices. He'd found a cleanish glass on the window ledge. The best way to avoid the taste was by pouring the cider under his tongue and swallowing fast.

"Sure you don't want a wee glass?"

The Wizard shook his head, eyes hidden behind the glare on his glasses. On his tray a new pattern of papers was covered in tobacco. He was plucking green buds from the plastic bag, sprinkling them on top.

Train in Vain came on and Nicky said, "D'you like the Clash?"

"You'll get hung round these parts, if you say you don't. Know what I mean? But it's beginners' punk. No offence, man. Anyway, if it's less than seven minutes, I forbid myself from listening. I took an oath."

"But this is only about three."

"Doesn't count since I didn't put it on. Sid's banned me from his stereo anyway."

Nicky drained the glass. He refilled it and picked up the bottle. "Think I'll go downstairs."

The Wizard saluted.

He took the stairs slowly, seeing the tops of heads huddled around the hall. By the front door Glove leaned and spoke with a girl. He'd matched his nail polish with a bit of black smudged around his eyes. Nicky wandered over.

"Nicky," Glove said, "you met Melissa yet?"

The girl turned. It was the Nazi Witch, in different boots and a short black skirt.

"Hi."

"Are you the Messiah?" She grabbed his jacket and kissed his cheek. "You're at my school, aren't you?"

Nicky nodded.

"It's full of arseholes and pathetic wankers."

"We've got more," Glove said.

"Ours is worse. All day I get called a mosher bitch. Even some of the manky wee first years chuck stuff at me."

"Mostly I get called a poof. Or a wee fuckin' gay poof. Or AIDS boy."

"That's just the truth though, Glove," she said.

"Except for the AIDS part," Glove said.

"Have you ever been tested?"

"You better hope so."

She rolled her eyes at Nicky.

Melissa was holding an empty glass. He lifted the cider and said, "D'you want some?"

She winced at the bottle. "No thanks. But thanks, you're sweet. Don't you think, Glove?"

Glove smiled.

Nicky looked into his glass then took a long drink. He walked off down the hallway, past a photo knocked from the wall, frame sunk in the carpet. In the picture a wee boy rested his head on a grey-haired woman's shoulder, her laughing so hard her eyes were gone and her face cracked with wrinkles. He peered in the living room. Folk were packed in, sitting around on the floor. The mist of fag smoke made him blink and rub his eyes, and he realised Glove and Melissa were watching from the end of the hall. Tip-toeing over arms and legs, he went in and found a space in the corner. Music blared. He sat cross-legged, and a long-haired boy turned to pass on a joint. Nicky shook his head. The boy pushed it under his face. Cardboard curled up in the end, damp with spit and lipstick smudges. He pinched hold and handed it on.

A boot came from above, crushing his pinky. He snatched his hand away, looking right up Melissa's skirt. She was kicking folk out the road, clearing a space, then she sat with her mouth close to his ear.

"Is that cider working?"

"D'you want some now?"

She shook her head.

Nicky took a drink and she closed her hand round the bottom of the glass. She tilted it and shouted, "Take your medicine."

The cider filled his mouth. He gulped and tried to pull her hand off. More poured down his throat. He gulped again. Some dribbled around his lips, spilling on to his jacket. She wouldn't let go, her other hand tipping his chin till the glass was finished.

He wiped his face on his sleeve.

"All done," she said. She put her hand on his knee and leaned in. "D'you like this?"

Nicky stared. Her mouth was wide and her lipstick black, sticky looking.

"The music?" she said.

He put his mouth to her ear. "Who is it?" Wispy hairs tickled his face.

"Korn," she said, "Have you never listened to Korn?"

"I'm more into punk."

She laughed. "I'm getting us some voddy." She used his knee to hoist herself up. Her skirt brushed his head as she went to the door, booting bodies out the way.

People gathered at the table. Crystal tumblers had been taken out of the glass cabinet in the corner and lined up and filled with bright red shots. A countdown began. The long-haired boy with the joint was there. He chucked his down at seven and the rest copied, slamming their tumblers back and hissing at each other. Folk started edging away, stepping on Nicky's hands. There was a crush in one side of the room. He got up and peered over shoulders. Space had cleared round a clammy-faced girl in stripy tights, hands covering her puffed cheeks. She doubled over and the tumbler rolled away, dribbling red across the carpet. She pressed her mouth and heaved. Folk groaned and cheered but nothing came. She let go and gripped her knees, gulping breaths and he thought he heard her groan and say, "I just ate sick."

Someone called his name – he heard it in the gap between songs. From a door across the room Fadge's sister signalled at him. He edged towards her. When he was near she took hold of his jacket, pulled him into the kitchen.

"Annie," he said.

"Come on." She led him out the backdoor.

Shadows cartwheeled at the bottom of the garden, walled in by big shaggy hedges. Everything had been left to grow wild and the concrete slabs were cracked. Annie sparked up.

He said, "How come you don't just smoke inside like everyone else?"

"Manners. And so I could save your life. Once again."

"How?"

"Melissa."

He put his glass on the doorstep and started filling it. "D'you want some cider?"

"Mibbe you didn't want saved though."

"I was just sitting there. She came over to me." He swallowed a big mouthful. "It's roasting in there though."

"Try taking that jacket off for once. Every time I see you it's done up to your chin, like a fuckin' straight jacket."

He pulled the zip down a couple of notches. "Is that better?"

"That's twice I've rescued you now."

"She was just getting a drink."

"So she could get you pished. She likes deflowering virgins."

Nicky took another gulp.

"She thinks she's a witch." Annie dropped the cigarette, most of it unsmoked and ground her foot till tobacco was crushed into the patio. "I'm away in," she said.

Everyone came into the living room to watch. Sid had set the kit up all wrong, as if Nicky was a left-hander. FUCK TRUMPETS had been felt-tipped on the bass drum, TRUMPETS written too big and too far along and squashed against the rim. Nicky had to reset the whole thing, hands sticky with sweat. Sid's eyelids were heavy and he swung his guitar in front of the speaker, filling the room with feedback. He kept shouting, "Messiiiiiiiiiiaaaaaah, can we fuckin' play now?" Fadge leaned on the mantelpiece with his bass on and his bottle of wine.

Nicky took some quick sips off cider, left it on the window ledge and picked up the sticks. He nodded.

"So play," Sid said.

"What song?"

"Who cares."

"How should I start it?"

"Just play, you lovely wee bastard."

He shrugged and started knocking out a beat, watching his feet work the pedals. Sid took his time lighting a cigarette and let it hang from his mouth. He swung his arm and hit a messy chord. Fadge lifted his elbow and left the wine on his amp.

Sid spoke into the mike. "LADIES AND—"

The fag fell out. He got on hands and knees. Nicky kept the beat going and Fadge turned for another drink, put the wine back, went towards the mike and stopped, glaring into the crowd. He started pushing through, the bass swinging. Folk shifted out the way and a tall lamp collapsed against the wall, bare bulb spilling light. Nicky kept playing. Fadge was pointing a finger and shouting, heading for a slick-haired boy at the back. The boy shook his head and raised his hands. His lips were moving, apologising. Fadge moved faster. Sid was still pawing around the floor.

A voice went, "TIMBER."

He tumbled over Sid's back, on to the bass and the lead stretched and tipped the amp face-first. Nicky stopped.

Fadge was sprawled out. "FUCK OFF. FUCK OFF YOU," he was screaming. His trouser leg was rumpled, one white sock stained with wine. The bottle was glugging away, carpet sucking up the red puddle.

The boy was gone. Sid stepped over Fadge and walked off, cigarette stuck in his mouth.

Nicky tried all the doors until he found Sid's room. The Wizard was on the bed in dimness, examining the end of a joint.

"Merlin," Nicky said, "been here all night?" He sat on the floor.

"Had a few visitors. One or two enquiries."

He put the glass and bottle beside him and lay back on the carpet, stiff and itchy against his neck. There was a voice sneering from the stereo. Guitars stabbed tinny chords.

"You still there Nick?"

He waved.

"How's the party progressing?"

"Fadge says he broke a rib. Someone tried to deflower me."

"You made it back though, man. I'm glad."

On the stereo the voice was going on about a Cadillac in a graveyard. The Wizard started singing along with the bassline, going, "DOO DA – DOO DA – DOO DA – DOO DA." He took some silent draws then said, "No one'll ever write a song as great as this again. Will they?"

Nicky opened his eyes. "I dunno. What is it? Probably not."

"D'you reckon there's some guy sitting in a bedroom somewhere, right now, with all these songs.

Even just one great song? Mibbe he's been too lazy, or unlucky, or some record businessman fucked up. Mibbe the guy didn't even write the songs or learn to play and they're just in there, unsung. But they're like the fuckin' masterpieces of our time and no one will ever have the privilege to hear the fuckin' things," he took another smoke. "When I say guy, I mean it also could've been a woman. Know what I mean Nick?"

"Kind of."

"It's weird man. It just seems to me that we got lumbered with the stick at the end of the shit." He laughed.

The band had stopped, leaving one guitar scratching between the chords.

"I might be that guy," the Wizard said. "Mibbe I'm the one. Or you." He turned up the volume.

The voice was gone. More and more notes came from another guitar, strung together till you realised each note couldn't be there without the one before. Nicky closed his eyes. It wandered on and on, tricking you into thinking it didn't know exactly where it was going. The band got louder and louder, the Wizard cranking the volume and it became one noise filling the whole room, everyone playing DUH DUH DUH, DUH DUH DUH, DUH DUH DUH, DUH DUH DUH. Eyes closed tight, Nicky banged his head against the carpet. The guitar broke free, climbing. It made it right to the top where no notes were left.

Then there was a harp. Something, not a human thing, crying. He closed his eyes again. For a few seconds it was only the drums.

Nightmare

Annie's face was there.

"I thought you'd swallowed your tongue. I knew someone who died like that."

"What time is it?"

"About half seven."

She was propped on one arm. Nicky sat up quickly and knocked the glass over. Cider spilled and they both rolled out the way. While he slept, someone had done the white outline of his body on the carpet. He picked at it. It looked like Tippex. There were two circles where the cider and glass were sitting.

"That stuff stinks," she said.

He turned away, hiding his breath, "Who died?"

"What?"

"Who swallowed their tongue?"

"No one really. But you hear about it happening to loads of folk," she stood. "You coming?"

"Where?"

"I've got a fucker of a hangover. You probably do too. We need medicine."

Nicky pointed at the stain on the carpet. "What about this?"

Annie rubbed it in with her boot then went towards the door. He got up and followed.

"Catch yous two later," the Wizard said, his eyes red slits.

He could see his breath. Overnight it had rained and the ground was soaked. On Sid's street most of the houses hid behind massive trees, pale dry semi-circles on the pavement below. Annie had a green army jacket on with a wee flag on each shoulder, the arms too long so only her fingertips poked out. She said, "When you're out this early on Sundays it feels like the world's ended."

"Where do we get the medicine?" Nicky said.

"Feeling rough?"

He nodded and she smiled then stared ahead, serious again.

She didn't speak until a jogger overtook. "Poor bastard," she said, "Imagine that was your life."

She looked at Nicky but he didn't know what to say.

They turned off the main road at the garage. Nicky stepped ahead and pushed the door open for her.

"Are you from the olden days?" She went in and told him to wait.

He asked if she needed money.

"You can get it next time."

A blue carrier back hung from her arm. She came out and marched past, the tail of the army jacket almost reaching her knees. He caught up with her on the pavement.

"You get all your stuff from Sid's?"

He stopped and tapped each of his pockets and nodded.

Annie watched. "Fuckin' hell. How many pockets d'you need?"

"I've got the same amount as you."

"My mum used to sew mine up when I was wee. I'm making up for it." She swung the carrier bag at him. "You've just got a shit jacket."

Nicky tugged it down. "Leave it alone."

She led them to the pitches and over to the play park. On the way past he nodded at the grass field. "Remember when that was all red ash?"

"Before I came here."

"Where were you before?"

"Fuckin' Wales."

"You don't have an accent."

"Thank god."

They sat on the swings and she started digging through the carrier bag. She brought out a glass bottle. "Hangover cure part one. Drink."

It was cream soda. He took a mouthful and groaned. "Too foamy. I think I might be sick."

She dropped a packet of crisps in his lap. "Part two. Eat."

"I hate cheese and onion."

Smiling, she reached for the bottle, clamped it between her thighs and rummaged in her pockets.

Nicky munched a handful of crisps, swapped back and washed it down with more soda. "I don't know if this is helping."

She held up a cigarette. "This is part three. Key ingredient."

"I don't smoke."

She smiled again and sucked on it.

They nudged back and forward on the swings. A few dog walkers passed in welly boots, dogs unclipped from leads and bolting for the tracks through the woods down to the river.

"What happened with Fadge last night?"

"The band sounded a bit shit. No offence."

Nicky tutted. "Sid's fault. Don't even know what he was playing."

"He started bevvying about eleven in the morning someone said. And Merlin's weed's pure super powered."

"What about Fadge?"

"Dunno. He's a lightweight."

"I mean – was that the old drummer he was going mental at? Shanks?"

She nodded.

"How come?"

"I thought you were supposed to be in church or something?"

"What time is it?"

"About half eight."

Her fingertips were wrapped round the chains on the swing, the nails painted a purplish colour with flecks picked away, white and pink underneath. She noticed him looking and stuffed her hands up the sleeves.

"You ever done a nightmare?" she said.

"Will it make me feel better?"

"You might spew, which probably will. Lie under my swing."

"The ground's soaking."

"Don't be a gayboy. Your jacket'll keep you dry."

"Quit slagging it. It's Gore-tex." He did as he was told, lying on the spongy surface. "Will this hurt?"

"Only if I fall on you." She spread her legs so he could lie in between then hopped on the swing. "You can do me after."

Feet on the seat, she clung to the chains and the black rubber swayed above his eyes.

"What's scary about this?"

She kicked her feet and got some momentum going. The swing went higher. It fell further each time and the seat sliced closer past his face. She went so high the chains slackened and the swing jolted right above his forehead, almost skinning his chin on the way back.

"I think I am about to spew. Stop, please."

She laughed with her mouth open.

"Come on. It's my turn."

The swing flew by, almost snapping his jaw.

"No fuckin' chance."

When he managed to open his eyes he could see her grinning, watching him. Smooth white skin bunched beneath her chin. Her lips were their natural colour and cracked, a bit of charcoal make up above her eyes.

He'd stood for a long time in the shower. His skin still felt greasy, the stink of cider seeping out. He tapped the drums, not bothering with fills. During the sermon he almost drifted off and Janet Johnson had to hiss at him over the piano.

While he was packing away the kit he felt a squeeze on the shoulder.

"You look like a zombie," Ruth said. She was wearing a tight jumper and stood close, rubbing him lightly.

"Thanks."

"You're all black under the eyes."

He nodded.

She tilted her head and smiled at him. "Why don't we do something this week? Feels like I've not seen you properly for ages."

"I'd like that."

"Well call me."

She did a wee hop on her toes and walked up the aisle to talk to someone else, her new boots on. He sighed and puffed at the mess of drum parts and cases on the floor.

VCR

He stepped over the outline at the bottom of Sid's bed.

"Sorry about that," he said.

"My mum's raging. She's talking about getting a whole new carpet. Even though it's been rife with jizz stains for years."

One white arm was stretched out.

They sat on the couch. Sid took the *ARMY OF DARKNESS* video box from the window ledge and started building. "Good party but. Fadge says his ribs are buggered and he can't breath properly. He's got a big carpet burn down one side of his face, like fuckin' – what's his name."

"Is that why we're not practising?"

Sid shook his head. "My mum banned us. Since the house got trashed."

"Should I go?"

"Nah. She likes you for some reason. Fadge is forbidden – that's what she said, but she called him Gordon."

Nicky nodded. The drum kit had been left in a mess in the corner of the room, drums stacked on each other and cymbals balanced on top. "How come Shanks came?" he said.

"Bastard knew he wasn't invited. Annie says he wanted to apologise."

"Annie did?"

Sid concentrated on the joint. When the hash was heated and crumbled into the tobacco he said, "By the way, I got us a gig at the scout hall. Headline slot."

Nicky picked up the lighter and flicked it a couple of times. The flame wouldn't catch. "Have we got enough songs?"

"Aye. We have."

"I only know about three."

"We've a couple of weeks, man."

Sid licked the joint and sealed it, scraping a few brown strands off his tongue. He started a CD with the remote, sat back and sparked up. "Never headlined before. Once we've done that we'll gig in town no bother."

They were watching themselves in the mirrored wardrobe. Nicky poked his fingers through his hair and pushed it up. "Think I'd suit your hairdo?"

"If you weren't going bald, aye."

"Get lost. I'm not."

"You just got a massive forehead?"

He held his hair back tight and brushed it flat again. "I'm not."

"Shave it all off man. You'd look quality."

Nicky took the lighter, trying again to get it lit.

"Don't wear the flint out," Sid said, eyes closed.

He put it back on the table and picked up a CD case. There was a cartoon weasel on the cover, wearing a leather jacket, cigarette dangling out its mouth. *SCREECHING WEASEL* it said across the top. He flipped the lid, closed it and put it back.

Sid watched through slit eyes. "What d'you think, man?"

"What?"

"The CD. It's on the now."

Nicky listened for a second. "It's awright."

"Just awright?"

"D'you like it?"

"I'm asking you."

He thought about it. "It's good."

"They're total rip off merchants but."

"S'pose."

"I love it though."

"Yeah."

"By that I mean it's a load of shit," Sid said. "I hate it."

Nicky reached for the case again.

Sid grinned. "I'm winding you up Messiah. Say what you think. Don't just go along with a daft arse-hole like me."

Nicky nodded. "Okay."

"There's good shit and there's bad shit. And there's in between shit." He sighed. His eyes were closed again. Between smokes he aimed the tip at an ashtray sitting by his side, ash flaking all over the couch.

Nicky asked him, "How long've you and Fadge been mates?"

"Years, man. Hated the big goon when I first met him."

"Has Annie always hung about as well?"

"When she got a bit older. But she used to look totally different."

"How come?"

Sid opened his eyes and ran the earring through his ear, smoke trailing around his head. "I dunno man. She wasn't like one of us lot. She had this long hair and dressed pure different. Wee skirts and white tights. But she was dead young, it was all wrong. Then one time she tagged along with Fadge to a party here, her hair all chopped off. Dyed n'shit."

"Seems like a good laugh."

Sid took a couple of deep draws, then tapped the joint tip down, killing the smoke and slotting the remainder in the ashtray. He sat forward and said. "I think it's time for the main attraction." He reached under the couch and brought out a shoe box.

"What is it?"

"Wait and see man."

He lifted the lid. There was a pair of crumpled school shoes. The slip-on kind with no laces. He dug beneath them, under a layer of balled-up tissue paper and took out a video. No labels. He handed Nicky the box and slid on his knees in front of the wee TV. When he came back he aimed the controller. The screen fuzzed and hissed.

"You need to see this."

He flipped a panel on the remote and the video started.

"This bit goes on for ages."

Lines zig-zagged across. He tapped again and the picture slowed. Sid nudged him. His legs spread and one knee rested against Nicky's thigh. The picture froze.

"What d'you think of Pammy?"

"What?"

"Pammy man, d'you like her?"

Nicky shrugged. "S'pose so."

Sid turned, their heads close on the couch. When he grinned, his cheeks folded over, deep dimples like gills. "Remember her video?"

Sid got the picture moving again. Grainy pink filled the TV. There was a couple on the screen. She had the camera.

"The Wizard got me it," he said. "He's a pure pervert."

Sid thumbed the volume button. The green bar appeared, flashing over the penis filling the screen, pumping in and out of Pammy. He held it until two notches were left and you could barely hear them grunting and gasping and the filthy words. You couldn't see the tip but it was huge, inches of flesh with muscle and veins clumped underneath. Did other people, folk like Danny Donnelly or Mack, did they go around with cocks so colossal?

Nicky held the shoebox with both hands. He hugged it into his lap. "How long does it go on for?"

"I dunno, man. Never made it the whole way through."

Sid's knee still dug into his thigh. Screeching Weasel played on the stereo. He looked away at the mirror and saw the reflection of skeleton poster, laughing through its smashed-up grin.

Pictures

It started raining half way round the circuit, thumping down and soaking his T-shirt till it sucked against his skin.

"This is torture. Pure fascist shite," Sach gasped some air. His hair was drenched and dripping on his steamed-up glasses. He dipped his head, feet scraping the ground. They were his brother's old trainers, he said. They were a size too big. His arms were limp and folded against his chest. "Am I meant to breath in with my mouth or nose?"

Ahead, Pete ran next to Jennifer Black. He was too busy fooling around, talking at her and bumping her shoulder and he stumbled over a kerb. She rolled her head back laughing. Dirt splashed her legs and her PE shorts were sodden and riding up her arse. Pete got down on a knee and fiddled with his shoe-laces, letting her get a few steps ahead.

Sach stopped and doubled over, hand shoved into his side. "Fuck it. Not meant to be doing this. Got asthma."

Nicky stopped with him. "You should give in a note."

"Did. I told you, teacher's a fascist. And a racist."

Pete and Jennifer Black disappeared down the hill.

Sach nodded. "Go ahead, if you want."

"Can't abandon a comrade."

"How come you're not running with Pete? You always did."

Nicky shrugged.

"Yesterday he was at the shops. Sucking up to Danny Donnelly and all his pals. I saw him lend a fag to Purdy. Pure Stockholm syndrome."

"Weird."

"Think yous two'll get a divorce?"

Nicky elbowed him. "Come on."

Once he'd paid for her ticket, most of the paper round money was gone. The place was dead. Someone was sweeping up a heap of spilled popcorn and a muted TV hung from the ceiling. Ruth watched. It showed a trailer about a wee boy's dad dying and being re-incarnated as a snowman. The snowman was sledg-ing through a snowball fight and two snowballs hit his chest and stuck there like tits. His coal eyes bulged. Ruth grinned, dark hair tied slackly so some hung either side of her face.

"So obvious he'll melt at the end."

She tutted. "That's a wee shame."

He held up the tickets.

"You didn't have to," she said.

"It's fine. I'm loaded."

"You didn't even want to see it."

"If it's garbage, you can pay me back."

"But you're going to hate it."

"Next time I'll pick something manly and you can pay."

She laughed and said, "Manly."

He flexed a bicep.

She squeezed it through his jacket. "Nothing there."

"Show us yours then."

She did the same, her arm bare.

Nicky pressed. "You are pretty butch."

"And you're a wee weed." She dropped her arms and snaked one through his. "Will we get popcorn? You need to keep your strength up."

Paying for the popcorn emptied his pockets. Ruth took his arm again and they strolled towards the screen.

"You might like the actress, she's a hotty." She reached and dug out a handful.

Nicky pulled the box away. "Not till the trailers start."

"Get lost." She stuck her tongue out, showing him the mashed up popcorn and squeezed his elbow into her side.

A buck-toothed boy from Nicky's school examined their tickets without saying anything. He made a wee tear and handed them back.

"Come on," she said. "Best seats are at the back."

The adverts played and they sat nudging each other's elbows off the armrest between their seats. She tossed bits of popcorn, trying to catch it in her mouth. It bounced off her face and she laughed. After the trailers, the room darkened and she sunk into the chair and rested her knees against the one in front.

The film was about Death. Death turns up in a tuxedo to kill off an old English actor but ends up falling in love with the old actor's daughter. In one scene Death loses his virginity to the daughter. Ruth took Nicky's hand and whispered, "Told you she was hot."

For a while they sat hand in hand. Then Ruth let go and rubbed her palm on her jeans and reached into the cardboard tub. She ate and put her arm back on the armrest. He nudged it and it slid off and lay by her side. Her face was transfixed. He left his hand close.

She'd been crying. Words scrolled across the screen and she sighed and the sigh turned into a yawn. She stretched so her hand brushed the back of his hair, stopping at his neck.

"So what happened to everyone else in the world?" he said.

"What?"

"When Death was busy getting his end away."

She pinched a clump of his hair. "That's gross."

"Was there a few days when no one died? In the whole world?"

"There was probably another one going about."

"Like a supply teacher?"

"You're so infuriating."

She moved her fingers. They were icy on his neck, and he flinched and shoved her away.

"I forgot how tickly you are." She went for his ribs.

He squirmed and grabbed her arms. The armpits on his t-shirt were damp. She laughed and the lights came on and she was sitting forward facing him while his fingers made loops around her skinny wrists.

Smiling, she said, "What'll we do now?"

Ruth was shivering and blowing into her hands. She wore a few silver rings, her nails painted with clear polish, and the tips white and neat.

"We could wait inside," Nicky said.

She made baby steps across the car park and leaned into him. "Warm me."

He tucked his hands up his sleeves, wrapped his arms round and rubbed her back.

"It's been nice to see you," she said.

"I know."

She slouched and her head rested on his chest.

"It feels so easy."

He nodded, her hair ruffling under his chin.

"Sometimes I get this feeling that I'm going round living like half a person," she said. "At school. I'm not very good at being me, I mean the me who I'm meant to be. I can't get the two parts to, like, click together. Does it make sense?"

"I think so."

"You're so cosy. This jacket smells of you."

"Is that good or bad?"

"It just smells like you," she sighed. "Do you have doubts about it?"

"About my jacket?"

"About everything. God. Mack says it's okay and it's important. There's the guy in the bible that says, "Help me with my unbelief." Like you can't really fully believe until you've had the doubts."

A car was coming. At the roundabout it swung round, away from the cinema.

"Sorry," she said, "I'm just blabbering."

"It's awright."

"It's what I mean, though. I don't know who else I would talk to like this, without worrying what I was saying because I was afraid or whatever."

"I wish we were at the same school."

The heat from her breath came through his clothes.

"Then we'd see each other every day."

"I'd be in the year above." She lifted her face and smiled. "I wouldn't be caught socialising with your sort."

He smiled too. He pulled her even closer, closed his eyes and aimed his smile at hers. She tensed. The rubbery skin of her ear rippled past and he tasted hair. He'd left his mouth a wee bit open. Headlights lit up the empty car park and she shrugged his arms off. They stood side by side, the car speeding towards them with its grill and slanted lights making a sneer. You could hear the muffled sound of a Paul Weller CD blasting inside, her dad chewing gum with one gloved hand on the wheel. Nicky tugged his jacket down. She'd left him with an agony erection.

He glanced over his shoulder. Behind the glass door the buck-toothed usher was watching.

Black Golf

Pete had moved to the desk behind, beside Danny Donnelly and Purdy and the boy with the chunk out his ear. They were meant to work in pairs but there was an odd number.

"Boy wonder can manage himself," Rubberfud said. He coughed into his hand and put it in his lab coat pocket. He ran his lip over his moustache and left the class, mumbling about seeing the technician.

Something bounced off Nicky's desk. He didn't turn.

"Boy wonder," Purdy said.

Pete whispered.

Purdy put on a woman's voice, "Jesus loves you, boy wonder."

Something else hit the desk. It was a manky bit of rubber rolled into a ball. He flicked it on the floor and concentrated on the diagram in front of him.

"Kum ba yah, my lord," Purdy sang. "Kum ba yah."

The rest of the class were quiet.

Pete joined in. "Kum ba yah, my lord. Kum ba yah."

"Sing it, Jesus boy," Purdy shouted.

A piece of the rubber bounced off his head. The boy with the chunk out his ear laughed.

Nicky kept his eyes on the desk. He rested his forehead against his hand.

"Must be busy doing his prayers."

The three of them started again: "Kum ba yah, my lord. Kum ba yah."

Rubberfud walked back in. He coughed into his hand and two of them stopped. Purdy kept going.

"Oh lord, kum ba yah."

He walked over and slammed the hand hard on their desk. Purdy shut up. Nicky glanced over his shoulder. Rubberfud stood jaw clenched, glaring down with his fingers spread on Purdy's jotter.

When he moved away, Purdy went, "You're a big peedo, Rubberfud. Everyone knows."

"It's Rutherford," he said. He never shouted. When he did his stammer came out.

At the top of the steps, a squat nurse watched the black Golf pull into the car park. She emptied a bucket over the banister and went inside. Mack guided the car into a space and switched the engine off.

"Sorry about this, bud. I made a promise I'd look in on someone."

"D'you not have any mates your own age?"

"Very funny."

When they reached the counter, the wee nurse was working her finger down a sheet of paper, muttering numbers. She raised the other hand in a halt sign. They waited while she stared at the sheet, tugging loose red skin around her mouth. Mack tried to tell her who they were looking for, but she made the halt sign again. She lifted the phone, held it to her face then hung up and clasped her hands on the desk.

"Yes?"

He gave her the name and she tutted. "Been up to his old tricks again."

They both shook their heads.

"New medication?" Mack said.

She took them down a curving corridor, numbered doors on each side. Flowers shrivelled in vases beside a few of the doormats. A door was open. Inside an old man sat in pyjamas, gaping at a tiny telly. The nurse peered in, and the man turned and gave them a gummy smile. She shut the door.

The corridor led to a room set up with chairs and coffee tables. She put her hand to the switch, then changed her mind, leaving them in the gloom. Light shone from the corridors at either end and out a hatch in the corner. She showed them to a cluster of chairs, halting again.

"You can wait here. I'll go fetch him."

Mack went for a low, cushioned chair, chewed up sponge bursting out the corners. He dabbed at a dark triangular stain on the fabric and chose a plastic school chair next to it instead. Nicky picked the same type opposite.

"Stinks in here," he said.

"Keep your voice down."

"I meant of cooking. Not—"

Mack shook his head.

The place was roasting. Sweat rolled down Nicky's ribs. Mack tugged his scarf loose and shoved the hair off his forehead. He fanned his face then jumped to his feet, grinning.

"Here he is."

The nurse was leading over a massive old man,

slippers scuffing and arms dangling. She stopped him in front of a leather armchair and put a hand on his shoulder. He wouldn't budge. Mack pressed on the other shoulder and the old man buckled into the seat, bent forward so you could see his full head of hair, thick and white.

"Just you be your usual charming self, Joe," the nurse said and walked off.

Mack leaned close. He crouched to meet the man's eyes.

"Mr Clayton. Hi. How's things going? Nicky here came to see you as well. Remember Nicky from the church?"

Mr Clayton lifted his big hands and slapped one on each thigh and puffed a long breath out his nostrils.

Mack turned an ear. "What was that?"

Through the hatch in the corner dishes clattered and taps gushed on. Mack leaned back, watching the old man. He scratched his head, raising his voice over the noise. "So Mr Clayton. How's the singing going? Still managing to fit in the daily practise?"

He moved his mouth, making a soft click with his tongue.

"I still reckon you could've taught Frank a thing or two."

No reply.

"Nicky here's a musician too." Mack nodded and gestured.

Nicky aimed his voice at Mr Clayton's ear. "I'm a drummer."

The old man blinked.

"He's not deaf," Mack whispered. He sat back,

reaching for an abandoned scrabble board and straightening some letters. Mr Clayton sighed, fingers scissoring the crease on his grey trousers.

Mack pushed the hair back off his forehead and blew some air across his face. He reached for a folded up newspaper next to the board.

"What about the crossword, Joe? There's a few clues left here," Mack said, "a biggie – 'One who studies butterflies and moths.' Thirteen letters. There's a T at the end there and a D and P in the middle. Any ideas?" He slapped the paper against his thigh.

Mr Clayton had frozen, staring at the floor like a sad old statue.

"What does it start with?" Nicky said.

"I'd have told you that, wouldn't I? Ends in a T so it must be some kind of ist. Come on Joe, give us a hand."

"Ist," Nicky said.

"It's on the tip of my brain."

Mack counted some spaces. He muttered to himself. His mouth opened and hung there, then closed and he leaned back, folded the newspaper and replaced it.

"Don't have a pen anyway."

For a while they just sat. A radio played from the hatch, every now and then a voice picking up a line of the song. Nicky swung his chair and yawned, and Mack gave him a look.

Eventually he checked his watch and stood. "Well. Time we let you get back to your peace and quiet I think," he laughed then turned to Nicky. "Wait here, while I find the nurse."

"I'll go."

"D'you even know where she is? Just wait."

When Mack was gone Mr Clayton raised his head. He had an ogre's face, with greenish skin and the end of his nose lumpy with growths. His eyes were a red mess of burst vessels. Nicky smiled. Mr Clayton shifted in the armchair and let out a long fart. It rasped across the leather seat.

"Nice one," Nicky said.

The big hands were fumbling in his pockets. He brought out a paper napkin and a short red bookie's pen. Nicky held a sleeve over his nose. The napkin was covered in rows of tally marks. Mr Clayton sniffed, adding a shaky I to his score.

"D'you remember him?" Mack said.

"Sort of recognise him."

"He did a lot of caretaking at the church. Way before my time. You'd have seen him when you were wee, cos he practically lived there. Kept that place running."

Nicky popped the glove compartment then pressed it shut. The black Golf always smelled brand new.

"There's a story that he caught a cat burglar in the church once – decked the guy. You can tell he was a big man in his prime. So he ends up sitting on this burgular's chest and the poor sod can hardly breath. Mr Clayton gives him two options. He's either going to call the police or they both sit down together and do a bit of reading. Obviously your man chooses the reading. This's all happening in the middle of the night. Mr Clayton heats them up some soup and pulls out one of the wee slim Luke's gospels. You know the ones in the cupboard with yellow covers? The two of them end up reading the whole thing. He explains it to the guy, does a wee bit of preaching and by the time the sun comes up this burglar's been converted. He's a legend, old Joe. Probably wiser than most folk that stood in the pulpit."

"How come he's in there?"

Mack shrugged. "That's where some folk go."

They stopped at the lights. A car pulled up in the next lane – spoiler sticking out and windows tinted black like Mack's. It revved its engine. Mack revved back.

"He read the bible front to back every year of his life."

"When was the last time you read the whole thing?" Nicky said.

"I'm constantly reading it, bud; every spare moment. What about you?"

"Yeah. Sometimes."

"You've gotta do it." He eyed the other car, the pair of them nudging noses back and forward.

"It's part of your job," Nicky said. "You get paid to do it."

Mack grinned. He'd swapped the black Golf's steering wheel for one out a racing car. A wee silver cross pin was pushed through the middle.

The lights switched to amber and he spun off. The other car matched him, heading for a line of parked traffic. At the last second, it veered and cut in front and slammed its brakes, red lights flashing. The black Golf screeched. Nicky jerked against the seatbelt.

Mack watched the other car speeding away, fingers tight round the steering wheel. Behind them a car blasted its horn and Mack muttered and restarted the engine. They drove off.

Further on he said, "Not long till you get your license, eh? Mack's taxis'll be out of business."

"Not for a bit. We don't have a car anyway."

"You ever tried?"

"My mum doesn't do it anymore. When I was wee, I got to sit on my uncle's knee on the beach and do the steering."

Mack nodded. They drove on to the next junction and he made a quick right turn.

They were in the old industrial estate. He stopped at the kerb and clicked on the inside light. "No time like the present."

"Can we not just get a drink or something?"

"Come on, bud. I was desperate when I was your age."

"I don't even know how the gears work."

"It's just like on your bike. And you'll be coordinated, from the drums," he tapped Nicky's leg. "Come on. Swap."

Mack explained how to work the pedals. Find the biting point. When Nicky tried the car spluttered and stalled. After a few shots, Mack said, "You're right. You are pretty terrible at this."

Nicky turned the key and eased the pedal in. The needle brushed the 3 and fell back, then climbed, touched the 3 and shuddered in place.

"Lift the clutch," Mack said. "And sit back. You look like an old woman."

The car edged forward. Nicky froze, staring at the beams lighting up the pot-holed road. The kerb curved and he steered with it, needles rising and the black Golf starting to whine.

"A bollard's coming up so you'll have to turn the car right round. The road's wide enough bud, so just go slow. And try changing gear before my engine explodes. Drop the clutch."

Nicky stepped on the pedal. He waved around for the gear stick.

"Watch it. Just turn gently. Watch."

He wiggled the stick into second. His trainer squeaked and slipped. The other foot kicked out and the car roared.

"Watch," Mack shouted. He grabbed Nicky's hand, throwing the steering wheel across. There was a bang. The car died. Mack swore. He tried to get out without undoing his seatbelt.

Two Girls

Sach was off.

At lunchtime he went to the top of the playground, towards the mound of grass where Sid and his pals smoked round the back of the dining hall. There was no one around, only two wee kids with legs dangling off the muddy verge and books open on their laps.

He wandered to the library. It was deserted. The

librarian frowned at him and stared back at her computer. In a corner mostly blocked by shelves he browsed through the spines, chose a book and sat at a desk.

Half a page later he heard a squeaking, rolling sound. He looked. Jennifer Black was coming towards him, books piled in her hands. Behind her a parked trolley was heaped with more. She passed, dumped the books on the floor and got on her knees. She slid to one side and propped herself on an arm. He heard the sound of her tights rubbing, glanced at her skirt riding high and shoes strapped to her feet with one buckle, a scuffed leather flower round the button. She turned. He was back in the book.

"Which comes first?" She was holding a hardback either side of her face. "They're both McSomething but this's got an A. This doesn't." She peered at it. "Mc."

Nicky pointed. She dropped them, thudding on the floor.

"You be careful with those," the librarian yelled.

Jennifer Black put her hands on her hips and climbed to her feet. She scowled at the books, spreading them around with a toe. She looked over.

"You're the Skelf's pal?"

Nicky nodded and stared back at the page.

She stepped nearer and crossed one leg in front of the other and put her hands on the back of a seat. She said, "How long've you two been wee bum chums then?"

He closed the book over his thumb. Close up you could see the powder brushed over her face, specked on the light hairs across her top lip. Her eyelashes curled, set stiff with black gunk blobbing between the strands.

"I dunno."

"Like, primary?"

"Nursery."

She laughed. "Tell us a story then."

"What about?"

Jennifer Black shrugged. "Whatever. Something to give him a riddy. He's always taking the piss out me for everything. He's a cheeky wee shit."

The librarian yelled from somewhere. "We don't use that calibre of language in here, thank you."

Nicky squeezed the book, crushing his thumb between the pages. He looked right at Jennifer Black's eyes, then blinked out the window behind her. She yawned. Both arms stretched to the ceiling, fingers linked above her head. She arched her back and her shirt strained at him. Yawn over, she said, "You got none?"

Nicky shrugged.

"Must be something you can tell me."

He looked around then leaned forward and started telling her. "He showed me this thing once. When we were wee. It was this thing you strapped round your belly." He held the book there, showing her. "For exercising the muscles."

"Like a stomach toner?"

"His mum kept it in a drawer under her bed. He took me in there and showed me it once. You strapped it on and turned the wee dial and it fired electric shocks at you."

"I know. Fuckin' hell," she whispered, but she was grinning.

"Right. Sorry. Pete took me in their room once and got it out the drawer. Then he put it on. Said he was going to give himself a six pack." He patted the book. "He straps it on and switches it on and turns it up full power and he—"

She frowned, lips making a wee grin, tongue between her teeth. "What?"

"He," Nicky let the book fall in his lap and flapped both hands downwards, "filled his pants."

"Shat himself?" She laughed and covered her mouth.

He grinned and nodded.

"You mean just a wee bit, or properly shat himself?"

"He bolted straight to the toilet."

"When?"

"I dunno. A few years ago. First year. No one else knows about it."

She laughed at the ceiling. "What a riddy," she said.

The librarian stuck her white head into the section, tapping her watch. "You better watch it young lady. Enough nonsense."

"Sad cow," Jennifer Black said when she'd gone. She crouched to the books again and built them into a pile, then looked up at him through her fringe. "That's not bullshit, it actually happened?"

"Yeah."

She smiled and went back to piling.

Nicky looked at the top of her head, the perfect line where she parted her hair. "I didn't know you liked all this."

"What?"

"The library. Reading and all that."

She didn't reply.

He left the library before the bell. Jennifer Black had finished in his section, gone back to her trolley and trundled to the next one. She was still there. The librarian looked at him from behind her desk and said, "She's not like us."

"What?"

"She doesn't care about books, like we do. You think she's here cos she wants to be? It's punishment. She was fighting. She's always fighting. Left a chunk of fingernail in some poor soul's face."

When he got there, his fingers were numb with the cold but the school shirt stuck to his skin. He'd phoned Sid to find out where to go, saying his cousin was buying a bass. Fadge might be able to help out. "I've seen the fat bastard put his bass on the wrong way round," Sid said. "I told you. He doesn't know shit about shit."

A few folk passed wearing the other school uniform. Nicky sat on a wall behind a hedge and peered up the street. His breath came back and his chest still pounded.

He didn't realise it was her until she was close. At the stop of the street, in her uniform, she looked like a boy out of first year. She made quick wee steps, eyes on the pavement, wearing grey trousers instead of a skirt. He took a breath and set off towards her.

"Annie."

She walked fast. She was halfway up the path when he reached her. The gate clanged shut over his voice.

"Annie."

She turned and gave him a look.

"Hi."

"What you doing here?"

"Is Fadge in?"

"I've not been in yet. Have I? Usually I'm first. Sometimes he doesn't get back for pure ages. Goes to the woods looking for pornos or something." She shrugged her school bag off and chucked it in the porch. Nicky stepped on the first slab of the path and took hold of the gate.

She came to the other side. "Did you come all the way from your school?"

"I was kind of passing. You awright?"

"S'pose. Usual shite day of schooling. You?"

"Fine. Yeah."

"You want me to check on Gordon?"

"I always think it's weird seeing folk in their uniform."

"I look about eight."

Nicky put his hands in his pockets. She rubbed her hair, messing it and pulled at a sleeve, stretching it over her knuckles. Her face was pale – dark circles under her eyes. A yawn came and she kicked a stone off the path. "I'll go and see if he's in," she said.

When she reached the steps she skipped the first and climbed the second then third and collected for her bag from the porch. She was almost at the door. He blurted her name.

She looked back.

"D'you want to do something?" he said.

"What, now?"

"Whenever."

"Not now. But I'm going to town on Saturday."

"This Saturday?"

She nodded. She had a hand on the door handle.

"Can I come?" he said.

"Do what you want. If you want, then meet me at central. One o'clock or something."

"Under the big clock?"

"That's where everyone goes. At the side, where the chemist's is. Should I get my brother?"

Nicky shook his head. "I can speak to him later."

"He'll be here soon," she said and turned through the door.

Friday

Something bounced off his shoe. He ignored it. A flattened can came next, splashing leftover juice up his trouser leg. He glanced over his shoulder. Pete waved from up the street. He wound his foot back and booted a lump of smashed concrete. It skited between Nicky's legs, bounced and smacked the brown-haired girl on the back of her calf. She shouted and went on one knee, both hands grabbing the dusty mark on her tights.

"What the hell happened?" the blonde one said.

"The wee shit kicked a stone at me. A massive one."

"What the fuck's wrong with you?" the blonde girl said.

Nicky went to point at Pete. He shrugged and said, "Sorry."

"Weird wee freak," the blonde girl said, she touched the other one's shoulder.

He overtook. When he was far enough away he turned, seeing her limp a few steps. Pete and Danny Donnelly waited, leaning on a wall. Pete was laughing.

"How'd you get on with Fadge," Sid said.

"Fine."

"Said you never turned up."

"I've not been yet.

"You coming tonight?"

"Where? I've got a thing on."

"Come on son. It's pub night."

"The pub?"

"Once a month. No more or we won't get in. It's fine, I know the guy. He's decent."

"I can't."

"Ach come on, Messiah. What you doing that's better?"

"What pub is it?"

"Tinto."

"They let you in awright?"

Sid tutted. "Everyone gets served at the Tinto. Don't be a boring bastard. Everyone's going."

"Mibbe next time."

"Suit yourself, boring bastard."

"Sorry. I really need to go."

"Yeah. Me too."

Sid hung up first.

The black Golf was revving outside. He looked out the window but the dent was hidden on the other side. The horn peeped again. They had to get there early to set up. After that there were the prayers.

Mack served. Nicky's team-mate returned the ball. The boy beside Mack hit straight into the net. He swore. Red acne was clustered on his cheeks.

"Now now," Mack said and served again. The ball bounced high and Nicky smashed it.

"Sorry."

The acne-faced boy stared. He touched where the ball had hit his Adam's apple. On his next shot he caught the net again. He chucked the bat after it and walked off. His friend waited, fingers digging under the loose rubber on his bat. Acne-face turned and looked and the other boy dumped the bat and followed.

"Why'd you do that?" Mack said quietly.

"Thought we were having a game."

"You've got to keep them amused. Especially him. Now they'll just sit around getting bored again."

"Not my fault he's rubbish."

"That's when the trouble starts. Be a bit more sensitive," Mack said. He tightened the saggy net.

A wee boy came over and challenged Nicky to a game on the ancient Atari. They were nudging squares across the screen, meant to be footballers kicking a smaller square when Mack walked up.

"Make yourself useful," he said. He laid a tape on Nicky's knee. Across the front it said HARDCORE

CHOONS in felt tip. "One of them asked for it on. You can be in charge."

He went to the stereo at the back of the hall, put the tape in and clicked the button. An electronic bass drum thumped and helium vocals joined in. He wandered back and restarted the game.

"That needs to go off." Mack was standing over him.

"I just put it on."

"It's not appropriate. You're supposed to check before you play it."

"It's a blank tape, Mack. There's been no swearing."

"It's all about doing drugs. Listen." He raised a finger next to his ear.

The wee boy put his joystick down and tilted his head.

"Switch it off and give him his tape back," Mack said.

Nicky shrugged. He went back and ejected it and slid in the Counting Crows CD.

Acne-face was coming. Nicky crossed the hall towards him, holding out the tape. The boy pushed past and the music stopped.

"We're not listening to this shite again." The CD drawer was open and he held the disc, fingertips at the edges.

"Can I have that please," Nicky said. "It's not yours."

"Give us the tape. That's not yours."

"We can't put it on. Sorry."

"How?"

"It's not appropriate."

"How?"

"It's just not allowed. Mack says."

"There's fuck all swearing on it."

"Give me the CD and I'll give you the tape."

The boy shook his head. "How come you're in charge anyway, wee bible-basher."

"You can't talk like that here."

"Let me put the fuckin' thing back on. Come on. Everyone hates this shite." He turned the CD and read the title. "Fuck off, Country Cows."

"I can't give you the tape till you let me have that. But you're not allowed the tape on."

"This place is a shitehole, d'you know that? For fuck's sake."

"So why d'you come?"

"To rip the pish out wee fannies like you. Give us it."

"No."

A grin cut up one side of the boy's face. "You're getting rattled mate. You've got three seconds."

"We'll have to chuck you out."

"Three."

He held the tape behind his back.

"Two."

"Look. Just—"

The boy took a swing. Nicky threw up his arms and ducked and the tape skidded across the floor. He blinked through his fingers. The fist hadn't moved. It hung in the air next to the grin.

"Fuckin' pussy."

Acne-face dropped his arm and walked off, laying the CD on the stereo. His pals followed. Nicky looked around, the group of boys barging his shoulders as they passed. Mack wasn't there.

The boys were in the lobby, heading out. Nicky pushed between the chairs stacked at the side, stamping on the tape lying there and crushing the plastic. Jacket off the peg, he shoved through the side exit and made it out the church before them.

The right bus sat at the stop across the road, engine rumbling. The doors hissed and he climbed on.

The fat bar woman didn't flinch, eyes on the newspaper spread out between beer taps. Sid was in the corner with a pint. He grinned and banged the space beside him.

"The Messiah is among us."

Nicky sat where a pillar hid him from the bar. "Where's everyone?"

Sid shrugged.

"I thought everyone was coming."

"Bastards bottled it." He took a glug.

Nicky pushed some coins across the table. "Can you get me one?"

"Go up yourself."

"Please. You're older. And they sold you already."

"There's only about one twenty there."

"D'you need more?"

"Fuckin' hell." Sid scooped the coins up.

Nicky slouched. A door at the other end of the bar opened and an old boy limped in. It was loud through there, filled with smoke and men sitting behind pints. The old boy had a tracksuit top on and silver stubble across his head and round his mouth.

He stopped at the fruit machine, swung his head and mumbled.

"What?"

"This paid out?" he shouted.

"I just got here."

He started feeding coins in and tapping buttons, bending till his nose touched the screen.

Sid slid a pint over, smearing the table and Nicky took a long drink and banged it down. The old boy looked over.

"Take it easy," Sid said.

Nicky took another gulp. "This beer tastes manky."

"Didn't know you were a fuckin' – what d'you call it? What happened to your other thing?"

"Didn't want to miss pub night."

"Could do with some tunes on but; it's fuckin' dead."

"Looks busier through that bit." He pointed at the door.

Sid shook his head. "You never go in the bar. Unless you want a boot in the balls."

"I thought this was the bar."

"This is the lounge. No one gets sold through there."

The bar woman coughed and gargled then turned her newspaper.

"I've got a tape with me," Nicky said, "We could get her to put it on."

"What tape?"

"*Insomniac*. Got it out the library."

"Come on son. Give up on that cartoon punk bullshit."

"It's good. You should hear some of the basslines—"

"No fuckin' way. Put that on and she'll definitely know we're unders. It's risky enough being out with you."

"What?"

"You look about fourteen."

"Get lost."

"D'you even shave yet?"

"Yeah." He swallowed more beer. "Just my top lip though."

Sid laughed.

"It's still shaving."

"What about pubes?"

"Do I shave them?"

"I mean have you got any, retard."

Nicky laughed. "Loads. What about you? Do you put as much gel in them?"

Sid downed the last of his pint. Nicky tried to copy, but only managed about an inch.

"Had to trim them the other day," Sid said. "It was like Jurassic Park."

"What?"

"Aye. Pure bushy."

"How'd you do it?"

"Just a wee set of my mum's nail scissors, man. Grab a bunch, snip and flush them down the pan. She goes nuts if I leave any wee floaters. Another?"

"I've still tons left."

"I'll go up. You get it dealt with while Jabba pours the next round." He nodded at the woman.

"S'pose," Nicky said. "I hate beer."

"You'll get used to it."

The old boy turned round. "Here," he said, "what fuckin' age are yous pair anyway?"

"Fuck off mate," Sid said.

He glared, took his glass from the holder on the fruit machine and limped through to the bar.

"Jakey bastard."

Sid was near the bottom of another pint, fag slotted in the ashtray. A mechanical noise kept churning in the ceiling above them, whirring silent then starting up again.

"Sid."

He turned away from the wee telly, showing a game show with the sound off.

"How come you've never been at the church again?" Nicky said.

"I hate that place, man. No offence."

"I don't care."

"It's my old man's thing. Him and my mum met there – and my old granda was there from when they built the fuckin' place. When my dad left, she quit it. Now I'm hardly ever at his on weekends. And plus he only ever goes, when he's wanting to repent. Dirty old prick." He smudged the condensation on the pint. "I was at his one Saturday night, and heard him with this wee bird – banging away. Some wee nurse he'd brought back from his work. I heard it all man. Him going to the toilet once they were done, then her tiptoeing in after. Cleaning their fuckin' parts. Then in the morning he was on his own. He knew I would've heard. He's got this shitty wee flat now." Sid looked up from twisting the fag in the ashtray.

"I couldn't stop listening to them at it. It was weird man. Pure grim." He made a quick laugh then drank.

"Did you ask him about her?"

He shook his head. "That Sunday he drags us both along to your church. Starts singing along to all your songs in his big gay voice. Nodding at everything the minister was saying."

"We don't have ministers."

"Whoever. They're fuckin' bores. You know none of the bastards are even listening. Then at the end they go about with the wee teas and coffees. Good morning. And how are you? Even the biscuits are shite. How can you be arsed with it?"

"You get used to it."

"You don't get bored?"

"I can't remember not going."

"Brainwashed."

"Get lost."

"Drink up son, you're miles behind."

The bar door opened, faces peering through. The old boy from the fruit machine limped in and pointed.

"Right yous two. Out."

A chunky barman came in behind, tea towel hanging over his shoulder. He looked over at the woman. "Margaret, what the hell you doing, serving these two? Look at the state of them."

"We're eighteen mate." Sid said.

"Fuck off." The barman pointed at the door and the tea towel flopped to the floor.

"Least let us finish these."

He closed his eyes, pressed his lips together and did a slow-motion head shake.

Sid pointed at the old boy, slumped against the doorframe. "You mate. You're a disgrace. A fuckin' grass."

The old boy grinned and waved two Vs like a band conductor.

Sid grabbed the pint and started downing it, beer trickling out the corners of his mouth.

"I'm not telling you again boys. Fuck off or it's the police getting called."

He gurgled through the beer. "Ach piss off mate."

Nicky snatched his jacket off the seat. It caught his pint and the glass wobbled off the table, smashing on the wooden floor. Sid laughed. The barman came over, veins forking up his neck and stopped over the mess. They were blocked in. He toed a loose shard towards the rest.

"Sweep that up," he said. He bent, his red face close to Nicky's and pointed at each word. "Fuckin' sweep that up."

"Thought we were getting the boot," Sid said.

"Margaret. Bring over that pan and brush."

At some point the barman had taken Nicky's jacket and it hung it his side, one arm trailing. The woman came over and put a metal pan and wooden brush on the table.

"I didn't mean it," Nicky said. "Sorry." He reached for the handle.

Sid knocked his arm away. "Fuckin' leave it. If we're going we're going. We're not sweeping any fuckin' mess."

The barman had calmed. "I'm telling yous. Sweep that up."

"Give him his jacket man."

He shook his head.

"Let us out, big meat head."

The barman laughed. "Who are you meant to be anyways?"

"Fuck you."

"You look like a shite Billy Idol son." He crossed his arms.

The mechanical noise churned in the ceiling. Nicky switched his eyes between Sid and the barman and the pan and brush.

"You can sweep it, Billy," the barman said, "then your wee pal gets his piece of pish jacket."

Sid shoved the pan off the table. It made a muffled thud on the carpet.

"I'm in no rush," the barman said. He folded his arms tighter. Above them the sound clunked off. The old boy still stood at the doorframe, eyes half shut.

The barman sighed and called over his shoulder at him. "Get Pelé out here."

"Pelé?"

"Aye."

"You sure?"

Sid made a step from behind the table. The barman moved closer, sealing him in. Behind, the old boy had gone to another door, STAFF ONLY stuck on the outside. He opened it and stuck his head in. "Pelé," he whispered, "Pelé," then backed tight against the wall, one stretched arm holding the door. There was a sound. A dog crawled out, small and low to the ground, short black fur like filth all over its muscly body. It sniffed around. The old boy watched and crept harder against the wall. Only a stub of its tail was left. The dog noticed the barman and its tongue flopped out. It ran over, eyes popping and red edged and its jaws grinning. When it crossed the wooden part of the floor you could hear the scratch of its claws.

The barman caught it by the collar and spoke in a baby voice. "Hey Pelé boy. Hey boy."

The dog was up on hind legs, scrambling at the air, panting hot stale breath. The barman's arm tensed with the strain. Sid had his wrists crossed at his crotch, one knee raised.

"Bastards tried to put him down three times," he told Sid. He rubbed a hand over the dog's head and down its snout and it snapped at the air. He bent and whispered something and the dog's ears flattened. It went still, hunched and the barman looked at Sid and whispered again. The dog's eyes bulged. A growl started in its guts and burst out the jaws in fierce barks, deafening in the quiet room. It was on hind legs again, lips peeled back and foamed with spit and Sid had both feet on the bench and his back against the wall, arms folded into his chest.

"Look. I'm only holding on by one finger," the barman said.

Folk had come through from the other bar, laughing along with the old boy.

"I'll do it," Nicky said. He was pressed in the corner, one foot ready to hop on the bench too.

"Shit."

The dog had its teeth round the rubber soul on Sid's boot. They slipped free and clamped shut.

Someone shouted from the back. "Go on Pelé boy."

"Fine. I'll sweep it. I'll sweep it," Sid said. "Get it off. Fuck."

The barman shouted over the barking. "What's that?"

"I'll sweep it."

The dog got one paw on the bench.

"Say sorry."

Sid was on one foot. "What. Fuck."

The dog had a hold of his trouser leg, shaking.

"Tell him you're sorry."

"Sorry. Fuck sake." He shouted, "Sorry Pelé."

The dog shut its mouth. It got off the bench, four paws on the floor and the growls stopped. Its eyeballs stayed fixed on Sid and the barman rubbed its snout again and it licked his skin.

Sid had the dustpan in one hand, brush in the other. He crouched. Nicky and the barman and the dog watched. Nicky asked for his jacket and he tossed it on the floor. Men from the other bar shouted.

"Missed a bit, son."

"Get the boy a wee maid's outfit."

When the glass was swept Sid put the pan and brush on the table. He glanced at the barman and back at the floor. The barman smiled at the pan then pointed where the dog had been standing. It sat and yawned. Breath wheezed in and snorted out its solid body.

"Pelé says you've to clean that up n'all."

A thick dark-coloured turd was curled on the bar floor.

"That's that fucked then."

Sid had dragged over a giant tyre that looked like it came off a tractor. They sat, the grass behind the scout hall long and wild and trampled flat.

"Sorry," Nicky said

"I fuckin' hate dogs."

"We should tell someone."

"Who like?"

"Police."

Sid made a laugh. "Shitehole anyways."

"Sorry."

"What are you even apologising for anyway? You didn't squat down and do that fuckin' shite, did you?" He tutted.

"Should of just swept the glass though."

Sid was staring into space, sniffing the tips of his fingers. "Don't tell anyone."

"I won't."

He sighed and popped the buttons on his jacket pocket and brought a half bottle of vodka.

"Where'd you get that?" Nicky said.

"I was giving the pints a wee turbo."

"You were spiking my drink?"

"I was spiking mine too son, calm down."

"That's why the beer tasted manky."

"I improved it. And plus you wouldn't be that steamin' otherwise."

"I'm not."

"You are a bit Messiah." His frown relaxed and he made a wee grin. "It's good."

Sid unscrewed the bottle and pushed it into Nicky's hands. He took it and drank a mouthful. His face screwed up.

"Rank, eh?"

Nicky spat. "Does all vodka taste that bad?"

"You never tasted voddy before?"

"Why do folk drink it? It's stinking."

"They pour coke or something all over it. So you can't taste it and it gets you pure pished. We're doing it the proper way. Like fuckin' Communist soldiers."

Nicky nodded. In the garden next door a security light had come on and he read the label. TOTOV VODKA.

"Or total tramps." Sid said.

Nicky took another drink, spat and gave it back.

"What a dick. That barman. Imagine being his age and stuck in that shit job. Fuckin' loser."

"What'll you be doing when you're his age?"

"God knows man. I'm fucked. Failing everything. My mum's trying to make me go to all these tutors after school, but it's too fuckin' late. I'm saving up for a van. Once I get my license, I'm taking the Fuck Trumpets out on the road. We'll get a deal with a tiny wee label and just make records and tour non-stop." He drank and handed it over. "Rest of that's yours."

Nicky waved his hands but Sid forced it. He took a sip and said, "You'll have to start doing your own songs."

"Got them."

"So why're we always doing covers?"

"Got to learn the skills, Messiah. Like the Beatles in Germany."

"Didn't know you liked them."

"I don't. They're shit." Sid shrugged and sighed. "Imagine, just getting steamin' and high and playing music. Meeting new folk every night. Not having to worry about some stupid house or idiot boss. You just keep going till you die. You up for it?"

Nicky finished the vodka and hissed. "What about a wife. Kids n'that?"

Sid laughed. He grabbed the bottle and stood.

"We should play your songs," Nicky said.

He was away, strolling across the boggy ground to the front of the building. Nicky tip-toed behind, trainers soaked. They went up the concrete ramp and out to the street and Sid threw the bottle at the scout hall. It hit the wall and shattered on the path.

Nicky laughed. "It's been a smashing night."

"You must be the only dick in the world that gets less funny when he's pished."

The black Golf was waiting. When he got close, the door swung open and Mack got out. "You can't just do that," he said.

Nicky stopped.

"You can't walk away like that. It's not on. You've got responsibilities now."

"Sorry."

"We all have to do things we don't like. Can't just bail when they get difficult."

"Sorry. I need to go in."

Mack squinted. "Where were you anyway? I've been here for ages."

"Better go in. It's late."

He started up the path, stumbling on a slab and into the gravel. Mack called his name in a stern voice but he kept going, climbing the stairs. The car door slammed and the engine started but the black Golf didn't pull away till he was safe in the house.

He flushed the plug to drown out the retching and splatter. Toilet water kissed his face. Staying on his knees, he stared at the vomit floating on the surface like a jellyfish and listened to the water refill. When enough time had passed he pulled the plug again, watching the last stringy parts get dragged off the bowl, sucked out of sight.

Town

Annie waited where she said she'd be, makeup darker round her eyes and her lips pale pink and glossy like icing. A long scarf was wrapped round her neck and stuffed into the army jacket.

"Bloody freezing." She shivered.

"At least it's dry."

"Later on it's going to rain." She leaned on the chemist window, tugging her bag strap.

Nicky said, "Will we go?"

"Where to?"

"I don't mind."

"D'you want clothes?

"Think I'm awright for clothes."

She shook her head. "Where d'you usually go? Marks and Spencer?"

He stared at her.

"I'm kidding. Where d'you want to go?"

"I just came in cos you were."

She straightened up. "Come on."

It was damp in the streets and she was right, it probably would rain. They passed a bunch of boys at the exit holding skateboards, chains looped from their jeans. One of them shouted her and she waved. "Coming to the steps later?" the boy called out. Further on she told Nicky they couldn't even skateboard, just carried the things around all day.

"Are you in here a lot?"

"Depends. Used to do dancing classes on Saturdays, but I chucked it."

He grinned. "You went to dancing?"

"Yeah. So. Started when I was wee."

"Were you good?"

"Fuckin' amazing," she smiled and dug out a cigarette.

They waited at the lights. Nicky glanced, watching her cheeks sink as she sucked, a blotch of pink staining the end. "Where we going?"

"Somewhere good. We'll get you some good stuff."

"I don't need anything."

They walked on.

The shop had no sign, just smudgy windows showing a few headless mannequins. He snuck in front and pushed the door open.

"You're such a weirdo," she said and ducked under his arm.

It stank of old clothes. Behind the till a tattooed girl with a pierced face smiled. Annie made a shy wave, fingertips fluttering from her sleeve. She led him through to the back, stroking the rails of clothes on the way. Rows of old boots stood against the wall, scuffed and dusty, some painted with cracked flowers and at the back knee high ones flopping against each other. Nicky stopped and gazed. She came up behind, her chin brushing his shoulder.

"You want some boots?

He turned a trainer on its edge. "These are letting in."

"They're manky."

"Me and Sid were down at the scout hall last night."

"Look. These ones are good."

"They're pure knackered."

"You'll look good in them. What size are you?"

He told her and she peered behind the tongue. "Perfect."

They were black with eight lace-holes, like Sid's. Across the toes the leather was creased to bits. Some white splatters came off under his thumbnail. He balanced on one foot and crossed one leg over the other and untied the laces.

Annie nudged him. "Flamingo boy."

"Get lost you." He nudged back, got the shoe off and the boot on and started working on the other foot. She crouched, lacing up the first.

"They nip a bit."

She watched with her arms folded. "You're walking like you've special needs."

"I was just trying them out."

"They'll stretch. Get them. You look good."

"Not too chunky?"

Annie had started flicking through a rack of coats

fixed high up the wall. She yanked one by an arm till it tumbled off the hanger.

"Nicky. Try this."

She made him feed his arms in. The cuffs hung over his hands and the tail dragged on the floor.

"Sich heil," she said, "You look like a mad Nazi bastard."

It was roasting. The wool itched his neck. He started shrugging it off.

"Wait a sec." She backed in, shuffling her feet in-between and slipped her arms in next to his. "This belonged to one big motherfucker. Do it up."

He stretched the two flaps and fastened the buttons, the middle one right at her chest where her scarf was knotted.

"So hot in here."

She stepped forward and he had to go with her.

"It's boiling. And it stinks."

They stopped in front of a mirror. Tufts of her hair tickled his nose and he inhaled her fruity shampoo smell. Only her eyes peeked out, the jacket buttoned over her face. She was laughing, vibrating and her shoulder blades dug into his ribs. She was getting him hard. There was no way she wouldn't feel him jabbing in.

The coat tore.

"Shit."

He'd tried to shove his arse away. Some old brass buttons had popped off. They wriggled out and Annie bundled the coat and chucked it under a rail of faded jeans. She grabbed his arm, laughing silently and led him away, down the stairs to the basement. The stink turned to blocked drains.

There was no carpet, just plastic sheets spread out and taped up at the joins. A thin man sat in the corner with a book folded over in his lap. Sideburns reached his jaw and he had boxes and boxes of CDs arranged on fold out tables. Nicky walked to a section with PUNK scrawled on the cardboard and started flipping through. The man crossed his legs.

Annie had quit laughing. "Let's go," she said.

Nicky picked a CD out. "Is this good?"

"I dunno."

"It's the Descendents. You had that t-shirt with the picture on it. At the scout hall."

"You remember what I was wearing?"

He nodded.

"That's a bit creepy."

When he looked up from the song titles she was already climbing the stairs.

"Early stuff's better," the man said, uncrossing his legs. "Unless you're into that poppy shite."

Upstairs he paid the pierced girl for the boots and Annie went out and lit up. The rain was on.

"Aw," she said when he came out. "Wearing your new shoes home?"

"Got to carry these around with me all day now." He held up the trainers.

"Here." She gripped the fag in her mouth, took the trainers and fed them in the bin behind.

"Annie."

"What? They're done. No one'll call you shit for shoes anymore."

"Who called me that?"

"No one." She pulled her hood up. "Just one or two folk."

She stuck a chip in and gasped, puffing hot breath.

"D'you not want to go to the steps?"

She looked at him, mouth open.

"The steps the guy with the skateboard was going on about."

"It's pure boring." She chewed and swallowed. "And they're all daft wee idiots."

"He was acting like you're best mates."

"It's like you and Sid."

"But I like Sid."

"I meant the other way round."

He elbowed her and she slipped off the plastic plank. Rain was rattling off the bus shelter.

"What were you and him doing last night anyways?" she said.

"We went to the pub."

"Tinto?"

"D'you go?"

"It's a shithole. How's Sid?"

"Don't think we'll be going back."

"How?"

"Doesn't matter."

"What happened?"

"Nothing."

She stopped chewing and eyed him. "You know he's got an eating disorder?"

"What?"

"I think so anyway. Have you ever seen him eat anything?"

"He doesn't look that skinny."

"If you see him without his shirt. He looks like he's out a concentration camp."

"Has he seen you without a shirt too?"

"Yeah. Good one. How's the boots?"

He raised one for her to see. "Giving me blisters and my sock feels wet like one of them's burst."

"Nice." She crumpled her chip papers and let them fall on the ground. "Sid said he met you at that church."

Nicky nodded.

"D'you still go? Like, every week?"

"Most."

"Me and Gordon used to go, when we were in Wales. My mum sent us to the Sunday school – she wouldn't give out our fuckin' pocket money till after we'd been. This daft old Sunday school teaching bitch told me I was going to hell."

Nicky dug around the chip bag.

She sucked some grease and salt off her fingers. "How come you still go?"

He shrugged.

"It's awright if you're into it. Or is it you can't tell your parents to fuck off?"

He dropped from the plank on to his feet and stared into the chips. "No one makes me go."

"Right," she said. "Sorry." She slid up till they were close again. "So d'you think I'm going to hell too?"

"It's not really up to me is it?"

"You do then."

"Where d'you think you're going?"

"I think it's all a load of shite. It's just nothing."

"You die and that's it?"

"Just black, like when you turn the TV off. I don't mean black, I mean you're just gone. There's no more black or any colours."

He screwed up the empties, collected hers off the ground and went to the bin hanging by the bus shelter. When he came back he said, "It's weird. I sometimes wonder if I even want to live forever. I start thinking about it – time just going on and on and on, and I get this sick feeling. And once I've started I can't quit thinking about it."

"You'll be fine. All your pals'll be up there. Jesus might let you play drums in the band."

He lifted himself onto the plank and slid close like she'd done, watching his new boots swinging. "Why don't you come with me?"

"To heaven?"

"Church."

She grinned. "No thanks."

Rain hammered harder and they both peered through the dirty shelter at the sky. An old woman shuffled in with her shopping bags. She shook her head and tightened her plastic hood. "Not even my stop this," she said.

Annie frowned and turned away. Her hand appeared from a sleeve holding a pack of fags. She peeled the plastic, flipped the top and plucked one with her lips. She tucked the packet in a pocket and brought her lighter out. Once the fag was lit, the lighter stayed in her hand. It was metal, all the sheen worn off it. She smoked, flicking the wee lid open and shut.

"I like your lighter."

She held it for him to take. "Used to be my dad's. He doesn't know I've got it."

"Is he still in Wales?"

She nodded. "When we moved up here, that's when my mum stopped making us go to church. Probably gave it all up when he had an affair."

"I can't imagine you and Fadge going."

"To heaven?"

He sighed. "Church."

She peered up the road and tutted, stubbing the cigarette lightly on the plank, twisting till the smoke died and slotted it back in the pack. She grabbed his hand and took the lighter and stuck her arm out at the bus, fingertips poking from the sleeve.

Her head was pressed against the window, dozing. His stop was first. He tapped her and she turned, drowsy and blinking.

"This is me."

"Shit. Whereabouts are we?"

"Not far."

"I thought you'd chaperone me home."

"I can if you want."

She grinned. "Fuck off. You'd be no use anyway."

"Fine." He pressed the STOP button and stood.

Near the front seats he glanced back. Her head had dropped against the window again, dark eyelids closed. Chips had taken the pink from her lips and they'd gone almost blue in the cold. The lower one curled out – it always did, unless you managed to make her smile and she showed you her teeth, lined up small and white and glossed with her spit.

He edged back and squeezed her arm. "Want to do something another time, mibbe?"

Without opening her eyes she nodded. Her hair left swirls on the glass. The bus bounced through some potholes and stopped.

"But don't say anything to my brother," she said. "Or Sid. He'll go and tell him."

"We didn't do anything."

"He gets weird about stuff."

Boots

After spreading the newspaper he forced open the polish. Rust stuck to his fingers. He skimmed the brush over the broken black surface and worked it into the leather, adding extra across the toes and digging the bristles in. He made both boots dull, none of the weak bulb in the basement reflecting. With the other brush he scrubbed until the sheen came through, spitting dots of saliva like he'd seen folk do and buffing it in. One hand inside, he tilted a boot under the light. The soles were big chunks of rubber, a wedge of heel worn away. The last person had probably died before managing to wear them out.

Beside him the shiny-faced boy had thrown his arms in a V, reaching for the ceiling with fingers spread and his eyes squeezed tight. He was balling the words. He must've been tone-deaf. On the other side Ruth swayed, a stray hand grazing Nicky's leg and her voice quivered, face screwed in some kind of agony. He stared at the words on the screen and moved his lips along.

The hall was full of folk from the other churches. He looked around, thinking he recognised the sick-eating girl from Sid's party. Ruth raised a palm to the sky and blocked his view. There were other faces from school, folk he never knew came to these things, folk he'd never go up and speak to.

The drummer hit a big fill and they sang another chorus, the band ceasing so it was just voices and drums. The worship leader let go of his guitar and clutched the air. Nicky's feet stewed in the boots.

They sang the final line. Long low notes bubbled from the keyboard and guitars plucked through chords. Mack returned to the front of the stage, eyes closed and arms out like a blind man. He spoke into his radio mike: "Lord. Bless this place. Each of these believers, gathered from all around. Bless this tiny flock, gathered from each corner of this side of your little city. Protect us and challenge us and send us forth into another week, ears ringing with the promise of the greatest flock gathered in your name on high for ever and ever."

A solemn amen went round the place. Then there was hush. They sat.

Ruth kept her head bowed and eyes closed. Folk started chatting, the hall filling with noise. She sat like that for a while then looked around, blinking.

"Enjoy it?" he said.

She nodded, tucking her hair behind her ears.

"Did you see my new boots?" He crossed one leg on his knee and tugged his trouser leg, showing her the whole thing.

"Watch it." Her cream coat was in her lap. She tutted and rubbed at a dirty mark.

"Sorry."

"How are they so scuffed already?"

"Got them second-hand."

She licked her thumb and rubbed at the dirty mark again.

"Means they're already broken in," Nicky said.

"Yeah. With someone else smelly sweat."

Nicky shrugged.

A girl walked over and tapped her shoulder. Ruth grinned, leaped up and the two girls hugged.

He looked away, eyes pointed ahead in case tone-deaf boy was sitting there, waiting to talk to him. He glanced. The seat was empty. At the end of the row the boy had both arms slung over the chair in front and his head burrowed in. He was shuddering, sobbing. Next to him Mack crouched with a hand on his shoulder and prayed into his ear.

He was first to leave. The smell of coffee wafted out the church kitchen into the hallway. He jogged down the steps and up the hill, teeth clenched and hood up and wee dashes of rain slashing his face.

Pete hacked up more gunk, spat in a hanky then scrunched it back in his pocket.

"Too many fags?" Nicky said.

He whispered back. "Lung infection."

"Nicholas," it was Fanny Pack, the English teacher, "If this was the real exam you'd be out the door. Automatic fail."

"I'm done."

"Well. Sit there and shut up. You'll need the practise for the exam hall."

He stared at the sheet. Pete kicked him. "Move your arm. I don't know any of this pish."

He didn't move.

Pete kicked harder. "Don't be a cock. Please."

Nicky leaned back.

"Your handwriting's shit."

"Nicholas," Fanny Pack said. Pink fat jiggled off her arm, finger pointing at the door. "Out."

"It was him."

"I don't give a damn. Give me your paper and get out. You were warned. Exam conditions."

"Unlucky," Pete whispered. "Grass."

"Peter. I've had about enough of you too. You can join him."

Nicky dropped the sheets on her desk. Her square glasses dangled round her neck on a stupid cord strung with tiny beads. She started raking around in her bum bag and took out her red pen.

He shivered against the freezing corridor wall, hands crossed behind his back.

"How long till the bell?" Pete said.

"I dunno. Thanks by the way."

"You grassed me up. At least you got it finished."

"It was easy."

"You're so keen," Pete said. He broke into coughs, specks of saliva spraying out and wet barks coming from deep in his chest. He hacked up a mouthful of phlegm and worked it round his mouth then swallowed.

"Should you even be in?"

Pete cleared his throat and smoothed his hair. It was caked in gel, combed flat and forward. His cow-slick flicked in the air, strands standing like spider's legs. Footsteps came along the corridor and he glanced and nodded. "Look who it is."

It was Sid. He waved with a purple sheet of paper.

"King of the moshers," Pete said.

He reached them and stopped. "Messiah. You're becoming a renowned troublemaker. What's your crime?"

"Trying to help him."

"Fuck were you," Pete said.

"Where you going?" Nicky asked.

"Just on a wander. Got this register I carry about in case any dick tries to stop me."

They could hear the teacher lecturing the class. Her voice came close to the door and Sid ducked. It moved away and he relaxed. "If anyone looks close I'm screwed. It's from last year. See?" He showed it to Pete. "Who's your teacher man?"

"Fat Pat Fanny Pack."

Sid grinned. "Tits so big they broke her back. I had the daft cow last year."

"You had her?" Pete said. "You rode Fanny Pack?"

He winced. "Imagine it, man. Would you?"

"Fuck off."

"If she gave you an A but, automatically?"

"Only if she kept the bumbag on."

Sid laughed. "She left her shopping bags in our

class once and we found this brand new bra inside. When she came back in, two of us were sitting there with it on our heads – one cup each. Fuckin' huge. She went schizo."

Pete laughed.

Her voice was droning on and on and another, fainter from the next class. Sid pointed at the door and spoke to Pete. "See when they're being pure arseholes, I always think about this: they've got to flap their mouths like that all day, every day, for about forty years. Poor bastards. Pure desperate for you to learn all the fuckin' necessary facts and information."

"Aye, or they're sacked," Pete said. He nodded at Nicky. "When we were wee, he wanted to be one. Used to have a dress-up gown and hat and this gay wee blackboard he'd write sums on."

"When I was about six," Nicky said.

Sid laughed and stepped over, turning the purple sheet for Nicky to see. "Look man. I've done the poster for the gig."

It was covered in biro scribbles. It said THE FUCK TRUMPETS in big black letters. Underneath he'd put FEATURING THE MESSIAH.

"You're the main attraction son."

Pete peered over Sid's shoulder. Footsteps sounded from round the corner and he gave him a tap. "Someone's coming man."

"Shit."

Sid folded the sheet, waved and jogged off.

"He's awright," Pete said. He pointed at Nicky's feet. "You copying his boots?"

Nicky moved to the other side of the doorframe and leaned there instead.

"Messiah," Pete said and burst into coughs.

Sid shook his head. "We can't be sounding this shit."

"We've not practised for pure ages," Fadge said. He tried to get the bass in tune.

"Have you even had that out its fuckin' case since last time?"

"So what man? It's the bass. Do you know how fuckin' boring it is to play on your own?"

"I've been practising. So's the Messiah."

"Course he has."

"You could at least get a new string, for God's sake."

"Count it in," Fadge said.

Nicky clicked the sticks.

"Aw. For fuck—"

"That was you."

"Bollocks."

"I got it right man. The second dot. Here," Fadge thumped the note on the bass. "That's what I played."

"A. It's a fuckin' A."

"Aye. So what did you play then?"

"It's shit. It's shit," Sid said and slumped on the arm of the couch. He twisted his earring.

Fadge unstrapped the bass and balanced it against the amp. It slid over, face first on the carpet.

"What you doing?" Sid said.

"Fag."

"No way. We've hardly done anything."

"Gasping man. And it's not like we'll get any better."

"That's why it's called a practise. Dickhead. We're headlining."

Fadge shrugged and put his lips over the fag. "Who cares man? It's just a piss up anyway."

"Gerry from Slack Grannies is coming down."

Nicky said, "Why don't we try something else?"

"Fag first." Fadge dropped on to the couch, one leg swinging over the arm.

"Lazy big bastard," Sid said. He swore at the ground and flattened his hair with both hands, dragging his fingers down his cheeks. He pushed his palms into his eye sockets and spat something and stamped on it. It was a mangled plectrum, chewed and squashed into the carpet.

"Sid," Nicky said, "we should do one of your tunes."

"Nah."

"What?" Fadge said.

"He's got some songs."

"Fuck off boys. Not in time for the gig."

Fadge blew a mouthful of smoke.

"We should just try it."

"Bob fuckin' Dylan."

"You're a pair of dicks."

"Just try it, Sid. It'll be good."

"Quit kissing his arse," Fadge said. He picked a 2p from the glass table and flicked it. It hit Sid's toe. "Give us a song Bob."

"I can't be fucked with this today." He unplugged the guitar and went out the room, the lead buzzing on the carpet.

Fadge was grinning. "He tried to get us to do his songs before man, they're bloody terrible."

"He might've got better."

"I'm not kidding. Total garbage."

Cross

He'd forgotten his watch. When his alarm clock screeched he'd switched it off and blinked and half an hour was gone.

Terrified wee first-years ran ahead, the pavement covered in leaves trampled to brown mush and set hard in the cold. The street behind was empty. Further on Pete and Danny Donnelly had stopped, sparking up. Purdy was with them. The first years ran past and Purdy clipped one of their heels, tripping the wee boy on all fours, school bag tumbling over his head. He got up and ran off, checking his palms. Nicky puffed air between his fingers and crossed the road. Pete was in a brand new red jacket, pulled in tight round the middle.

"Excuse me," Purdy shouted. "Excuse me," he said, sounding polite.

"What?"

"Coming over?"

"Why?"

"Just come over."

"We're late," he said and pointed at his wrist but Purdy waved him with both hands. Nicky dodged between the cars queued at the lights and balanced on the kerb at the other side. The three boys stared at him and he dug his hands in his pockets.

Purdy spoke. "Nice boots."

He lifted a toe and gazed at it then back at Purdy.

"I'm kidding. They're shite mate."

Danny Donnelly gave the boots a bored look, squinted at the sky and scratched his moles. Pete was sparking at the fag.

"Want a smoke?" Purdy said.

"I'm fine."

"Skelf says you're at that church near me."

"I dunno."

"The pure weirdo one. Happy clappy shite."

"Where d'you stay?" Nicky said.

Pete blew smoke towards him. "When he's not out with the mosher gang."

"Why the fuck d'you want to know where I live?" Purdy said.

"Probably wants to post you a bible."

Nicky shrugged. "I don't care."

"You're a state mate. They look like special shoes."

Purdy and Pete laughed.

Nicky made a pathetic smile and walked away.

"What you smiling at? Fuckin' Jesus boy. Come back."

Over at the fence, one of the mob went in his bag and pulled out a boxing glove. The rest crowded round. He stuffed his hand in and knocked the boy next to him on the side of the head.

On the wheel chair ramp, Sach sat with a crumpled timetable spread across his chest. It was covered in smudged pencil.

"Envision it on a T-shirt."

Nicky put his eyes close. "Still can't read it."

Sach tutted. "It's a logo. I'm changing the name of my combo. Henceforth."

"Who's in it?"

"Me and my wee cousin." Sach turned the logo on his lap and tutted again, brushing at it. "Wish you'd seen it before. It was an utter masterpiece. But my cousin made me change it. Said he'd quit and tell his mum, so I rubbed the whole thing out. Then I thought fuck it, I refuse to be censored, so I rubbed it out again and redid it. Then I kicked the wee shit out."

"What's it called?"

"Black's Bastards."

Nicky frowned. "You can't call it that."

"Yes I can. It's got an apostrophe." Sach pointed at the paper.

"D'you mean like Jennifer Black's?"

"Jennifer Black's Bastards?"

"Yeah."

"I suppose you could think that – if you've some weird mother fixation. That would be very revealing, young Nicholas."

"What are you on about?"

"You want to shag Jennifer Black, but you also wish she was your mother."

"Shut up."

Sach grinned and admired his logo again. "The newspapers'll hate it, so they'll print it all the time. With stars over Bastards and that's not even supposed to be the offensive part. Imbeciles."

The mob were taking turns thumping each other. One of them had a bit of blood dripping from a nostril and he was rubbing it on the back of his hand then his trousers, trying to grab his shot of the glove. He glanced behind. Eyes wide, he whispered something and they quit messing and huddled at the fence. The boy with the glove hid it behind his back. Purdy was coming. Pete tagged along behind.

"Bell's about to go," Sach said. "Time we returned to the misery?"

Nicky nodded and picked up his school bag.

Purdy had the glove on. He flexed his fist then smacked one of the mob in the eye. The boy blinked and put his hand to his face. He forced a grin and Purdy hit him on the other eye.

Nicky and Sach were away from the wheelchair ramp and almost round the corner.

"JESUS BOY."

The glove was thrown over the fence. Purdy was crossing the playground fast.

"JESUS BOY."

Sach made a sideways glance. "Keep going. Bell'll go soon and we'll be inside."

"JESUS BOY," Purdy went again.

Nicky stopped and turned. "What?"

"Wait up."

Pete was trailing and shrugged when Nicky caught his eyes.

"Meant to tell you something earlier." Purdy said. He took a step and bunched the neck of Nicky's jacket in his fist and twisted his knuckles. Nicky choked, Adam's apple jammed back in his throat. He hit the concrete and his head bounced, tipped over Purdy's leg. Purdy was kneeling over him, pinning his hands. Their faces were close. They were clasping hands. The smell of wet dog came off him.

Pete's face appeared. He was holding the marker.

"Do it."

"What'll I write?"

"Just fuckin' anything."

Purdy wet his lips.

Pete frowned, marker hovering. He coughed into Nicky's face then he was gone, barking hard in the background.

"Fuck's sake."

Purdy had the marker. Nicky managed to get a hand free and against his chest and wriggle away, but Purdy slashed and left a cold mark on his forehead.

He shoved through the crowd, the playground scrolling under his boots. Purdy was still on his knees. One of his trainers had come off. Pete was still coughing and hacking.

Water gushed out both taps and he threw it on his face and scrubbed. There were no mirrors. Sach came through the door and Nicky turned, tie soaked and flopping against his shirt. He was crying, but the water ran down his face and might've disguised it.

"What does it say?"

"I tried to pull him off," Sach said. "Honest. Grabbed his manky shoe but it just came off."

"What does it say?"

Sach peered. "I dunno. It's just a squiggle."

"Doesn't say anything?"

"I think it's meant to be a cross. Like a Christian cross."

Nicky scrubbed again.

Sach took a handful of paper towels and rubbed them on a grubby bar of soap. "Try this. If it doesn't work your fringe is quite long. You could brush it over."

Nicky took the towels.

"It's not as bad as pie."

Sach leaned against the door, blocking it.

He gripped the chains tightly, the swing barely moving. He let go and punched himself on the thigh. He was a drummer and his arms were strong. He could do some damage. It was always afterwards, you realised what you should've done. A knee in the bollocks and Purdy would've let go. While he was curled up and clawing his balls he could've battered him a few times. Bounced his head off the playground. There were wee sharp stones there. They'd slice Purdy's fat face.

Two women came near, pushing buggies with kids toddling along, podgy wee hands clutching the frames. He left the swings and walked away from the play park and disappeared through the bushes, down to the river. Sitting on the flat rock, he kicked at the gritty bank, straining through all the other sounds filling up the place and wondering if he'd hear the bell for home time.

Horses

Annie opened the door before he knocked. She was in a black vest, arms white and bare except for a black bangle. Pink socks poked out the bottom of her jeans. He smiled at her.

"Should I take my boots off?"

A door at the end of the hallway creaked. She shook her head, pulled him in and turned up the stairs. When she reached the top she went in one of the rooms and waited in the doorway. There were three other doors and ladder feet sticking from a hatch above. A photo of a dopey yellow dog hung on the wall.

Annie sighed. "You coming?"

He followed, breathing in perfume.

"Give me the jacket."

"Don't put it in the bin or anything."

She shut them in the room and hung his jacket on the handle. They faced each other. Clothes were piled in a corner. A bra strap hung from the middle like a tongue, pink with black edges.

"What you looking at?" she said.

"Just looking around."

She followed his eyes to some posters. "I need to take those down," she said. "They're shit that lot. I was into them years ago."

"I've still got this poster of birds up," Nicky said, "from some magazine when I was about seven."

She sat on the corner of the bed.

"It's got wee pictures of all the garden birds. I can identify a chaffinch for you."

"Handy," she said and gazed at her hands.

"Think it's the same blue tack from when it first went up."

He sat on the opposite corner. Annie was twisting the chunky bangle round her wrist, running it up and down her arm. She saw him watching and stopped.

"Looked a bit like I was wanking my arm, didn't it?"

Nicky smiled. He went over to his jacket and fetched the CD box out a pocket. He laid it on the bed between them. "I got this for you. When we were in town. It's the Descendents one."

She took it and turned it over then opened it.

"Thought you should have it, since you've got the T-shirt."

She said thanks and stretched for a wee bug eyed stereo beside her bed. Her vest rode up, her jeans hanging off her hips. Nicky got up. He went over to the board beside the door and looked at the jumble of things pinned there.

"You're a right wee nosey bastard, aren't you?"

"How many concerts have you been at?"

"Some," she said. She was nodding along to the CD and playing with the bangle again.

He pointed at a jotter open on the desk. "What's this?"

She rolled her eyes. "Jesus. Didn't know I'd be getting an inspection."

He smoothed the page and started reading.

"Get lost. Don't read that."

"I can't anyway. Your handwriting."

"Fuck off."

"What is it?"

"English. That poem – The Horses."

"We did it last year."

"So finish it if you want."

"It's about world war three," Nicky said, "And the horses come back."

"I know that."

"Sorry." He sat on the chair in front of the desk and turned to her, lifting his hair. "Can you see anything there?"

"What like?"

"Good."

"No, hang on." She moved along the bed and sat so her eyes were near his forehead. She sunk her teeth into her bottom lip and frowned. The lips were glossy pink again, with black drawn around her eyes. "I can mibbe see something."

He turned back to the jotter. "You've got this wrong."

"I told you not to read it."

"At the top you've put Edwin Morgan. It's Muir. Morgan's that other guy."

"I knew you were a wee smart arse. Let's see then. Move up."

"No room," Nicky said.

"Slide along, we'll both fit."

Nicky pushed the chair away from the desk and slapped his knees.

"Smooth," she said, but she sat all the same. "Where's this mistake then?"

He pressed a finger on the jotter. She ran her fingertip over the top of his hand, over the knuckle and down to the fingernail then looked at him and he was looking at her, faces close.

His knees went dead after a while. Their lips detached and she rubbed her neck and moved to the bed.

At first they faced each other, side to side. Then she took her mouth away, smiled and touched his shoulder, rolling him on his back. She put a knee on each side and sunk him into the spongy mattress.

There was no telling how long they'd been there. The Descendents had finished a long time ago. He opened his eyes and they were filled with her face, pink and blurred and his tongue ached and slugged around her mouth. Hers was soft and pointed, making wee figures of eight. The room was silent except for the sound their mouths made and their clothes rubbing. She was dragging herself up and down. He'd stopped worrying about the stiffy and pushed against her, fingers feeling under her vest and following the dents either side of her spine to where her bra crossed.

Their teeth clattered. He gasped, puffing air into her mouth and tensed. He didn't mean to shove her away. She leaned on one arm and stared.

"Need to go to the toilet."

He stepped into the hallway and clicked the door

shut, holding his T-shirt by the hem. He was about to peel it back and look.

"What the fuck are you doing here?"

One of the other doors had opened. Fadge stood there.

"GORDON. LANGUAGE," a woman screamed from downstairs.

Nicky stretched the T-shirt across his thighs and opened his mouth. Fadge shook his head. He went back in the room and slammed the door.

"GORDON," the woman yelled.

The lock wouldn't catch. He rammed with his shoulder, raised the door and slid the bolt it in. He undid his fly. Dots had seeped through to his jeans. He peeled back his blue pants and looked. Paper flaked off the handful of bog roll and stuck to the mess. His pubes were all matted. It stank. The elastic pinged back and the stain slopped against him and he yanked the jeans and blue pants off, standing there in his socks and T-shirt, the stiffy half drooped. The same dopey yellow dog grinned from a photo above the toilet.

He moved a pink razor from the bath edge and sat. The cold plastic chilled his arse and goosebumps spread across his thighs. There were wee hairs trying to sprout from the skin there. He picked at one of the red eruptions.

Jeans back on, he flushed away the bog roll and folded the blue pants and stuffed them in his back pocket.

Annie sat cross-legged on the bed.

"I thought Fadge was out," he said.

"He is."

"I saw him in the hall."

"Shit."

Nicky leaned on the radiator. "I should go."

She nodded.

"Are you okay?"

"Are you?"

"I'll stay a bit if you want."

"Do what you want," she said.

"Sorry. I want to. It's late."

He stopped at the bed and the mattress edge dug into his knees. Her eyes had dropped. At her crown there was a lick of real hair colour. It swirled, turning from brown to muddy to black. A wee tuft stood up. It always did. She picked at the covers, rolling bobbles between her fingers and piling them.

"Take your CD."

"It's yours," he told her. "I copied it on a tape."

The path followed the river, passing a short waterfall choked with junk then crossing the white bridge. When they were wee he'd tried to fish off the bridge with Pete. They'd brought a ball of string and a paperclip and found a worm but neither of them would pick it up. It squirmed away and they tried to stab it but the paper clip was too blunt.

Someone stood staring out at the water on the other side. You weren't supposed to shortcut through the park at night.

"Son." It was an old man. Mud was splattered high up his wellies.

Nicky nodded. He kept going.

The man called again and waved. "Honestly. You need to see this."

Standing there were three heavy horses, flares of hair around their hooves dipping in the shallow water. They had padded jackets strapped round their bellies.

"Should they not be in the stables?" Nicky said.

"They're having a rare old time."

Two were nuzzling at some long grass. The third stood twitching its ears, a sodden plastic bag caught on one leg.

"Should we tell someone?"

"I wouldn't know who. Not this time of night," the man said. "I mind a peacock escaped once and roosted on the roof across from us."

Two of the horses trudged on to the bank. The third was still twitching and gazing over. It lifted its massive head to the sky and huffed air out its nostrils then sipped at the river. It looked again and caught Nicky with its black eyes, flicking its tail. Shit plopped in the water behind. The horse turned away.

He went to go.

"Son," the man said. "Look. I've lost my dog. Can you give me a wee hand?"

"Whereabouts?"

He waved a flat hand toward the bushes. "Could be anywhere."

"I need to go."

"I'm not dodgy son, honest. I've no idea where it's went."

Nicky walked faster, cold air cutting through his fly and shrivelling his bare bollocks. He went to dump the blue pants in a rusty bin by the gate, then stopped and shoved them back in his pocket. All sorts went on in the park. Someone found a medieval mace once – it was on the front of the local paper. If some horrific crime happened the police would dig the pants out, his DNA stained all over them.

Narrow Path

Nicky hesitated at the corner. Sach nudged him. The boys were sitting on their wall outside the shop – Purdy, Danny Donnelly, the boy with the chunk out his ear and Pete. Sach gave him a full shove and they crossed the road.

Jennifer Black and her pal had come over. She stood in front of the four boys, hands on hips and one foot out on a heel. It was freezing and she only had a blue shirt on. Sach and Nicky went passed. No one spoke. Safe in the doorway, he heard Purdy's voice:

"Your wee nips are poking out like bullets."

Jennifer Black told him to fuck off.

When they left the shop, the girls were on the wall too. Jennifer Black had her arms folded tight and they were all waiting for Pete to unwrap his pack of fags.

Purdy looked, grinned and went, "Awright Jesus boy."

They walked on.

"Aw come back. Barry's wanting his ear healed."

"Fuck off you," the boy with the bad ear said.

"Mind that time in Primary," Purdy shouted, "when you took your favourite bible into school?"

Sach stopped. He turned and took a step. "Purdy, you weren't even at his primary."

Nicky tugged his jacket.

"Aye I know. The Skelf told me but."

Sach took another step and pointed. "Purdy. Mind that time in our primary? You got caught playing with yourself under the desk?"

Purdy stood.

"Even the teacher thought your cock was tiny."

"Come here."

"So you can get me with your micro penis?"

Danny Donnelly grinned.

"Fuck off you," Purdy said. "Wee fuckin' Paki."

Sach laughed.

On the way to the gate they didn't speak. Nicky glanced over his shoulder. Nothing happened.

Back in the playground he said, "You shouldn't noise him up."

Sach opened his can. "Who cares? He won't even be here next year, then what'll he do? The man has no prospects. He was awright when we were wee – I had to sit next to him in primary. He drew dead good pictures. Once we were doing R.E and he drew this one of Jesus being crucified without any pants on, just this crooked willy like a finger. The teacher went mental. But now he's just fuckin' pathetic."

He slotted his 50p in the piggy bank. Mack didn't look up.

"Didn't expect you tonight."

"Thought I'd come. Hope you don't mind."

Mack nodded and went back to filling in his sheet. "Ruth's in. You probably knew."

He found her playing table tennis with a bunch of wee girls. They were in a ring, hitting shots and running round the table. Ruth's go hit the net. She put her face in her hands and told them she'd lost her last life. The wee girls tried to make her stay, but she tugged one of their ponytails and wandered over.

"Fan club," he said.

"They keep giving me extra lives."

He glanced round the hall.

"They're not in," she said.

"What?"

"The boys from last time. Mack told me. He banned them for a month. Come on." She felt his sleeve and he followed her to the church kitchen. She opened a cupboard and took out two chipped mugs and a drum of chocolate powder, spooned it out and filled the mugs under the big metal urn.

"So where've you been all my life?" she said, stirring.

"Nowhere. What about you?"

"It's nice to see you."

"Yeah."

"Not seen you since the cinema. Properly." She eyed the liquid. Dark strands of hair fell from behind her ears. "The film wasn't that bad was it?"

She smiled and he smiled back.

"It was terrible," he said.

She lifted herself and sat on the worktop, leaning

against the closed hatch. Tea and coffee was served from there after services. A rota of women's names was stuck on the wall then a faded poster. "THE LORD PROVIDES" it said, big block letters hanging in a cloudy sky over a field of corn.

Ruth slurped from the mug. "No other news then?"

He shook his head.

"Sure you're not keeping secrets?"

"How?"

She slid back to her feet. "Doesn't matter."

"Right you dirty skivers," Mack walked in, a plastic hockeystick over one shoulder. "Ruthy please go and spare us from those wee girls. They're arguing over you. Trying to guess what colour your eyes are."

She closed her eyes. "What colour are they?"

He swung the hockey stick and tapped her stomach and she groaned and doubled over.

"See you afterwards," she said.

When she was gone, Mack rested the hockey stick by the fridge. "It's good to see you, bud. Glad you made it back."

"Ruth says you banned the boys."

"They haven't shown up, but yeah. If they do."

Mack went to say more then stopped and opened the fridge, took a carton of milk out and sniffed it. He put it on the counter, brought down a mug and dropped in a tea bag. He filled it from the urn and sat it by the milk.

"Is the car okay?"

"She'll live."

Mack lifted Ruth's spoon, sucked it clean and fished the teabag out, pressing it against the side and dumping it in the sink. He found sugar and added two heaps. Once he'd spun the lid back on he pushed the milk away and put both hands on the counter and spoke towards the hatch.

"I've gotta say, Nicky. We were disappointed, all the leaders. You left us in the lurch."

Nicky put the mug to his lips.

"And then finding you in the street like that," Mack turned, "drunk."

"I wasn't—"

"Let's not piss around here." He pointed the spoon. "You had a responsibility."

Nicky nodded.

"I know we're friends, bud, but I'm responsible too – for keeping you on the narrow path. It's what they pay me to do."

"I'm sorry." He slid his mug on the counter, glanced at the door and went to speak.

"Not yet." Mack waved him back with the spoon. "We're not done."

"What?"

"Tell me about your band."

Nicky waited.

"Got nothing to say?"

"What about it?"

"I've known for weeks. Your friend's dad told me. He was psyched about you joining, thinking you might rub off on his boy."

"Sid?"

"There's been a change in you since. Ruth thinks too."

Nicky kept his mouth shut.

"That boy – You know his mum and dad met here?"

"I think they got divorced."

"Sadly so. And you remember old Mr Clayton at the home?"

Nicky nodded.

"That's how his mum came here. Mr Clayton's your pal's grandpa."

Nicky frowned. He reached for the mug again and stopped.

Mack went on, "I didn't expect him to be that way when we visited. He's not like he was. Worse now. Your friend's not said anything about it?"

He shook his head.

Mack pushed the hair off his forehead. "I just want you to be careful. A band called – whatever it's called. It's not even the name that matters."

"Are you telling me to quit it?"

"Bud, telling you what to do – that is definitely not my job. I think you need to ask yourself – why's it been a big secret?"

"It's not a secret."

"Really? Cos I don't remember you telling me about it. Or telling Ruth."

"We've got a gig. Tomorrow."

"I know."

Nicky shrugged. "Come if you want."

"You've had so many opportunities. It's taken this for you to tell me. So maybe, deep down," Mack put a hand across his chest and sighed.

"I know."

"But if I can't talk to you then my job's pretty pointless." He looked at his watch. "I need to go, check up on these young reprobates. Pals?"

"Yeah."

"What?"

"Pals."

Mack put his fist out, waiting for Nicky to bump it with his own.

Fuck Trumpets

Glove dragged a metal stand into the middle of the back room. A flip chart hung from it, pages scribbled with notes from a first aid class. He flipped till he found a blank sheet and said, "Awrighty boys. Let's get this set list sorted. Sid, what's our opening number?"

"Fuck up, Glove."

"You can't talk to your manager like that."

Sid had shaved his hair to fuzz at the sides. A long strip was gelled up the middle. He climbed and sat on the old piano in the corner, feet on the lid and swigged from a plastic bottle. He had a black t-shirt on. The same skull from his bedroom wall grinned on the front.

"Why don't we write out all the songs we have, then put them in order."

"We don't do a fuckin' set list, Glove."

"You should. All the big bands do."

"You're not being our manager."

"Aw come on."

"I get us all the gigs. Get every fucker to come. What d'you do?"

"I provided the refreshments."

"Fuck off. The Wizard got that."

"I phoned him but."

"S'pose the Beatles' manager was a big woofter," Sid said. "They did awright."

Glove chucked the pen at him. He chose another from the tub and started drawing.

"How busy is it?" Nicky said. He doubled over, poking the drumsticks into his hollow stomach.

"Packed. You nervous, Messiah? Take a wee drink."

He shook his head.

"First gig we ever did Fadge got so nervous he spewed in Shanks's bass drum."

"Shanks is a dick." Fadge said. He sat in the corner with his bottle emptied, picking at scraps of label and staring into the plastic.

Glove stepped away from the board. "How about this then – I've come up with our T-shirt design." He'd drawn a pair of balls and a cock sticking straight out. Before the balls he'd put a trumpet mouth-piece and three buttons on top.

Sid grinned. "That is so shite."

Nicky started laughing.

"Here – it's good," Glove tapped the tip. "On a trumpet that bits the bell end too."

"Fadge. Come see this pish."

He shook his head and chucked the bottle on the floor.

"What's up, son? Got your period?"

"Fuck off." Fadge stood. "I'm getting a smoke. Coming?"

They watched him slam the door. Glove and Sid gave each other a look.

"What's up with him?" Nicky said.

"Let's just get the gig done, man. Fuckin' showbiz comes first."

There was a stink of burnt dust and it was too bright – the whole stage humming with light while out there it was dim and you could just make out their eyes, waiting. The CD faded.

"SHITE," someone shouted.

No one spoke. Sid's amp buzzed. He was fumbling, trying to slot the guitar lead in.

"SHEEEEEEEEEEEEEIIIIIIIIIITE," the same voice went.

Something rumbled along the floor. Glove was pushing the stand from the backroom across the stage. A circle had been added round the logo and FUCK and TRUMPETS at either side. Nicky checked the snare again, smacking it a couple of times. He tried the kick pedal, the place quiet enough to hear it squeak and reached to tighten the cymbals.

Sid turned. "You awright?"

Nicky sat again.

Sid faced the mike and strummed his guitar. He yelled the first line. He had something to say.

Nicky smacked the drums: BAM BAM.

The next line was about killing someone's baby.

The beat began. Fadge stood slumped against the side, but his fingers found the right notes. Nicky's boots gripped the pedals. The skin on his palms had healed over, hard. Folk were pushing near the stage.

Gerry from Slack Grannies was there, towering over everyone with a fist up.

They were at the second verse when Fadge came across. He'd quit playing and was tugging at the low rusty string. It was loose. Snapped. He tore it free and held it out for Sid like a dead flower. Only two strings were left. Sid glimpsed over his shoulder and shrugged.

The first thing he did was kung fu kick the mike stand. It lay there squealing. He unstrapped the guitar and took it by the neck and raised it above his head like an executioner. Out in the hall they cheered, pleading him to do it. The guitar smacked against the stage and the amp groaned. It was still in one piece. He did it again. Nicky got up and took the kit by the toms and shoved the whole thing over, kick pedal flipping and grazing his shin. Sid was stamping on the guitar. He jumped on the neck with both feet and got on his knees, tearing parts and throwing them into the hall. Nicky had the drum stool by the legs, playing the cymbals with the seat. Fadge was gone, the bass propped against the wall. Back on his feet, Sid kicked the wrecked guitar into the hall. He pulled his t-shirt off and stretched his arms out like a Jesus. The place went quiet, cymbals ringing dead. Then he turned and Nicky saw what Annie meant. Sid was skin and bones. Ribcage rippling out and stomach sinking. Across his chest it said in big black letters **KILL YOUR PARENTS.**

He placed the stool back. Mack was standing by the door, arms folded.

"Want me to go back for your bass?"

Fadge ignored him, sitting on the piano stool like a saddle. When Sid came through he said, "Good thing we did all the fuckin' practises."

Sid grinned. He went over to the piano and lifted the top. "Cheer up misery guts." He lifted out a bottle of wine and handed it over.

"What's this for?"

"Bass player of the year. And here," he brought out three fat cigars. Sweat blobbed round his hair and trickled down his face.

Fadge took one.

"Messiah. Take yours."

"I don't smoke."

"It's only a cigar man."

"I'm awright. Honest."

"Don't be a dick."

"Glove can have it."

Sid flung an arm round his neck and got him in a headlock.

"Get off."

"Open your mouth."

Nicky tried to push him away. "You're stinking. Get off."

"Open up, son."

"Get off—"

The plastic wrapping scraped his tongue. Sid pushed till he wretched then kept shoving. Nicky coughed and elbowed him. He elbowed again, harder and tugged his head free.

"Piss off, Sid," he said. The cigar was in his hand, damp with saliva.

Sid held his ribs. He let out a long breath and glared. "Calm it, man."

"It was sore."

"You don't have to be a fuckin' woman about it."

Fadge watched from the piano stool, half-grinning. Sid kept glaring, hands falling from his ribs in fists. On his skin the black letters were smudged and trailed with sweat.

"You were choking me."

"It was just a laugh. Jesus."

Sid went over to a plastic bag, shaking his head. He took out a clean t-shirt and draped it over his shoulder. "Do what you want. I'm just trying to include you. We just done a gig and we're supposed to be a fuckin' band. Everyone wants to be a Fuck Trumpet man, but only us three get to be it." He went to the door. "Fadge, let's get these sexy beasts smoked."

Fadge unscrewed the wine and took a gulp. He hissed and left it in on the window ledge.

When he was alone, Nicky reached and snuck some mouthfuls. His throat burned. He sniffed the cigar through the cellophane, and unwrapped it.

Glove was smoking at the wee set of steps outside. Annie and the girl Melissa were with him.

"Folk are asking for their money back," he said.

"You gave a wee guy a splinter," Melissa said. "They had to get the first aid kit."

Fadge looked at Annie. "I said you weren't to come."

She took a draw and stared back.

"Here – where's mine?" Glove went.

Sid had the cigar going, holding the flame over

the tip till it smouldered. He held the smoke in his cheeks then let it billow out. "Sorry son. Only for the talent."

"Give us a draw then."

Sid took another puff, blew the smoke in his face and shook his head.

"If you give me one draw I'll sell you my logo. Just one."

"Take the Messiah's. He's being a wee poof about it."

Nicky shook his head. "I don't want the logo."

Sid reached and grabbed Nicky's cigar. He bit the end off and spat into the grass and aimed it at Nicky's lips. "So you're smoking it?"

Nicky took it and looked at the ragged end.

Sid waved the flame, telling him to puff. He breathed in and heat filled his mouth. He tried to hold the smoke in. His lungs exploded. When he managed to quit coughing his mouth was scorched.

They were laughing.

"Tastes like burnt toast," he said.

Sid grinned. "Did you try inhaling?"

"I dunno."

The fag had barely left Annie's lips. She was starting on a fresh one and you couldn't tell if she was smiling or just clenching it.

"Here." Nicky handed the cigar to Glove.

"Messiah, that's a shite effort," Sid said.

"He can have a bit. I need to go and see someone."

"Who?" Sid shouted. "You don't have any other pals."

The black Golf was parked at the scout hall gates. Beside it Mack stood half lit by a lamppost, hands in his pockets and lips pursed. White breath spouted, as if he was whistling without making a tune. Folk were leaving the hall, passing round him into cars waiting with hazard lights flashing. Nicky waved and he waved back.

He was almost there when someone screamed and feet scuffed up the lane.

"GET THE FUCKIN' MOSHERS."

Sid and the rest were huddled behind the wee wall, wet splats dotted on the side of the building. Nicky crouched, in no-mans' land. An egg splattered off his shoulder and another hard on his ear. He crossed his arms over his head. Folk at the door were squealing and shoving back inside. The man from behind the desk stuck his face out, took a few steps and an egg belted the door. He ducked back in.

Danny Donnelly came round the corner first. Then Purdy. There were some others, then Pete following at the back.

"That's enough."

Mack stood, shoulders squared, blocking the pavement. Danny Donnelly stopped a few steps away. They were the same height. An egg came from behind and caught Mack's shoulder. He didn't flinch.

"No more eggs."

Another one flew, smashing on the black Golf's windscreen. He glanced behind. Danny Donnelly came forward, flicked his cap and the brim grazed Mack's forehead. Mack's hands hadn't left his pockets.

"Away you go and leave these guys be. Half of them are wee kids. You not got something better to do?"

Danny Donnelly laughed.

"Go on. Bugger off and let them enjoy their night."

Danny Donnelly moved slowly. He lifted an egg from the long carton and palmed it flat on Mack's head. Mack's neck sunk into his shoulders, yolk oozing down one ear and his hand came out fast in a fist and caught the side of Danny Donnelly's nose. There was no crack, just a clipping sound.

"For fuck sake," a voice went.

The carton lay open on the pavement. Danny Donnelly crumpled, face in his hands and a drip of blood between his fingers.

"Fuckin' hell. Who's this hero?" Sid was there.

Mack was in the black Golf. The engine running. It reversed and the windscreen wipers went on, smearing egg. The car steered out the space and drove off.

They'd gathered round Danny Donnelly, not touching him.

"You awright?" Purdy said.

Pete was peering from the edge. He only had a small box. The flap was open and his fingers felt one of the eggs. Danny Donnelly lifted his face, blood streaking into his mouth.

"Here." Sid walked closer, arm stretched over the wall.

Purdy stepped in front. Sid was offering a hanky. Danny Donnelly elbowed Purdy and took it, opened it and spread it across his face. He tipped his nose in the air.

"Stick your head forward," Sid said. "The blood'll go down your throat otherwise."

Purdy told him to bolt.

They crossed the grass towards the others.

"That was nuts," Sid said.

"Did they get you?"

"I'm too quick son. I saw your wee mate with them. What's he doing with that bunch of clowns?"

Nicky shrugged. "Sorry about the cigar."

"I'm just trying to make it a laugh man. D'you know how long I've been waiting to headline the scout hall?"

"Where'd you get the hanky?"

"My pocket."

Nicky grinned.

"It's a hanky. So fuckin' what? A good one."

Fadge was miles away, chugging his wine in the gaps between cars. The other four filled the pavement and left Nicky tagging a few steps behind. He poked around his ear for eggshell, the splattered t-shirt hanging out one pocket. He wore Sid's skeleton one, damp with gig sweat.

They turned off the main road. Fadge was out of view. Nicky moved faster and tapped Annie's arm and she slowed and let the other three walk ahead.

"You're not saying much tonight."

"Not got much to say," she said.

"What'd you think of the gig?"

"Yous only did about five minutes."

He glanced over his shoulder. "Fadge's being weird with me. Did he say anything?"

She shrugged.

He watched her arms hanging as she walked, thought about taking one of her hands or even squeezing it then letting it dangle. He couldn't see her fingers, as if her fists were balled inside her sleeves. She sniffed the air then looked in his direction.

"It's dried in egg. And sweat," he said. "But it's Sid's."

They crunched up the driveway. A curtain flashed then the door opened and Sid's mum stuck her head out. She shouted him, and he turned and shook his head at them. Glove held out a stick of gum. He took it, folded it in his mouth and went in.

"Bet she found out about the guitar," Glove said. "Someone phoned from the scout hall."

"Scout hall doesn't have a phone," Melissa said.

"Aye it does."

"Gordon used to get bullied at Cubs," Annie said. "Used to always phone our mum, pure crying and get her to come for him."

"See. Does so have a phone."

"You mean in Wales though," Nicky said.

They all turned.

"Fadge must've been in scouts when you were in Wales," he said.

"When were you in Wales?" Melissa asked her.

She shrugged, looked at her boots and ruffled her hair. "Here's the big freak now."

Fadge dumped the empty bottle on the wall. "Let's go fuckin' in. Freezing, man."

"Can't," Glove said, "He's getting a bollocking."

The door opened. Sid stood in his socks, blinking and chewing hard on Glove's gum. "Yous need to go."

"Did she hear about the guitar? Did he phone her?" Glove said.

"It's something else. I'll catch yous. Sorry." He pushed the door.

Back on the street Melissa said, "Where now?"

"I might head. It's not like we've got a bevvy."

"Stay, Glove man. Back to ours," Fadge said. "We'll get wired into my mum's peach schnapps."

"You refilled it with water last time," Annie said.

"She's got other shit she doesn't touch. We'll find something." He led the way then spun, finger pointing at Nicky. "Not you, you wee tit."

Nicky smiled.

"I'm fuckin' serious."

"What?"

"Gordon. Fuck sake."

"He can fuck off home. He's not coming. The wee rat's got up to enough shit in my house."

"Fadge, calm it man."

"If you are the fuckin' manager, then tell him he's sacked."

"It's not up to you. What about Sid?"

"Sid knows. He said after the gig we'd tell him. You were fuckin' there, Glove."

Glove faced Nicky and bared his teeth.

"This is awkward," Melissa said. She walked off, catching up with Fadge.

"He's just pished man. He gets like this," Glove said. He stood for a second then shrugged and followed.

Annie's head hung. One heel stood on the toe of the other boot. She went to go.

Nicky spoke. "Does he know?"

"What d'you think?"

"Everything?"

She frowned.

"I mean. What happened."

"I dunno. What happened?"

"I'm sorry."

"You need to quit apologising for every fuckin' thing. You're—" She tutted.

"What?"

She turned, digging in her pockets as she went.

Pete was sitting on the wall outside the garage, red jacket glowing under the lights. His head was in his hands.

"Nick."

He kept going.

"Nick. Come back." He was on his feet. Braces had been attached to his bottom teeth. He tightened his lips and spoke from the corner of his mouth. "Silly cow won't sell me. Says I'm not sixteen. Can't get fuckin' I.D for being sixteen."

"Are you pished?"

"Purdy sent me out for the fags and I can't go back without them. Go in for me."

"How's Danny Donnelly doing?"

"Says his nose's broke." He pushed out a creased fiver. "Please."

"Should've got more when you bought all the eggs."

"Wasn't my idea. I was just carrying them. And they taxed them anyway, mad bastards." There was a line of metal across his top teeth too.

"Whose cash?"

"Mine. Go on. I've been away pure ages. Jennifer Black's there." He swayed and sat on the wall again, holding out the fiver.

"She won't sell me either. The woman."

"You look older. You've always. Where you going anyway?"

"Home."

"Where's the moshers?"

Nicky put his hands in his pockets and turned away. Sid's stale sweat wafted under the jacket.

"Please," Pete called out. "For God's sake please."

He stopped at the corner and watched from behind the post box. A man had been walking the street behind him. He passed Pete and Pete's lips moved but the man walked on. Pete tapped his backpack. The man turned and took an earphone out, watching Pete wave towards the garage. He was tall and thin and had to stoop, holding a hand to his ear. Pete mimed a cigarette. Shaking his head, the man pressed his earphone back in and went to go. Pete took a step after him. He grabbed a pocket on the backpack. It gaped. A folder tumbled out and papers flapped from the folder on to the pavement. The man twisted round and a bottle fell from the open bag, blue glass shattering and soaking the papers. He looked at the mess and lunged for Pete.

He had Pete's jacket by the chest, pointing at the mess and yelling and Pete was limp, letting the man shake him around. A police car cruised past and blocked Nicky's view. It slowed, u-turned and parked. The flashing lights came on and they climbed out in their uniforms.

It didn't take long. There was a discussion. The tall man spoke and pointed at Pete and the police scribbled in notepads. One of them ducked, sniffing Pete's breath, him slouched on the wall. The man leaned in to Pete's face to say one last thing but the police put a hand on his chest and guided him away. He crouched, shaking his head and peeled the papers off the ground and smoothed them inside the folder. When he was away the backdoor of the police car was opened and Pete climbed in.

For a while it sat by the kerb, one of them twisted round in the seat with her hat off. The other stood outside, speaking into his radio and brushing the blue glass against the wall with the side of his foot. He got in and they drove away.

Knuckles

He smacked a cymbal. The congregation bellowed the words and he felt a split-second shiver. Janet Johnson looked over her music. She lifted one hand from the keys and crossed her lips with a bony finger. A deep hack sunk between her eyebrows. They were thin, vanishing eyebrows, drawn over with black pencil.

After the opening song a man in a short-sleeved shirt walked to the lectern and welcomed everyone. His bright yellow tie said AUSTRALIA in falling letters, surrounded by cartoon kangaroos. He was known for his ties. Gripping the lectern, he beamed around the place then studied his notes. He put the grin away.

"A sad announcement to begin. Some very sad news," he said. "Our dear friend and brother, old Joe Clayton passed away yesterday evening."

Tuts and sighs went around the place.

"Mr Clayton was this building's faithful servant. He'd been known to the church since, I think, the year it was built." He looked at a man in the front row and raised his eyebrows. The man's big grey head nodded.

"Yes indeed. Since the year it was built."

The funeral arrangements were announced.

The church rented a flat for him across the road. He searched for the name beside the buzzers but only saw yellowed slips of paper, ink smudged unreadable by leaking water. He was about to walk off but noticed the door sitting unlatched.

He climbed the steps, tiles broken, the close stinking of fag smoke and bleach and flowers dying on window ledges. Mack's door had a fish sticker above the letterbox, curling at the edges. His name was on a tiny card inside the doorbell.

"Nicky. Hi. Wasn't expecting you."

"Sorry."

Mack held the door half open. He peered around the close and said, "Got some visitors this afternoon."

He waited.

"But pop in."

Nicky closed the door and followed, Mack's

slippers dragging along the worn brown carpet. He went in the kitchen and Nicky leaned, watching him stare into a mug and trail a teabag around.

"Tea?"

"Is that the first time you ever missed a service?"

"Feeling pretty rough." He sat the teabag on the rim then let it flop back in.

"Did you hear about Mr Clayton?"

Mack nodded.

"Thought you might be upset."

He sighed, toed a wee pedal bin open and dropped the teabag. "It's sad. But it's a good thing he's at peace. How's your friend?"

"Not seen him."

Mack tipped milk into his mug. The red stamp from the scout hall was smudged on the back of his hand.

"Sorry about last night. What happened I mean," Nicky said.

He'd gone in the fridge. His hand held the edge and you could see red across his knuckles too. He closed the door. "Think he'll be upset? Your friend?"

"About last night?"

"About losing his grandpa."

Nicky shrugged.

"D'you think he'll regret it? His antics?"

"He was just having a laugh."

"Behaving like that while the old man was passing away. I'd feel sad."

Mack took a drink and put his mug down. He rinsed the spoon under the tap then dropped it with the mound of dishes soaking in brown soapy water.

"Y'know the guy with the eggs," Nicky said. "He's from my school."

Mack perched against the sink and sipped. "You looked like a different person up there. I didn't recognise you."

"Didn't think it'd be your thing."

"Well."

Car engines whined from a TV in another room. A frantic commentator shouted. Mack listened. The voice calmed and he took another drink.

"Your band Nicky, it's just about destruction, the whole thing. Don't you think?"

"It's just a laugh."

"Just a laugh. What's good about destruction? Or funny?"

"I dunno."

Mack tutted. "When are you gonna get serious?"

"I don't think I'm doing it anymore anyway. The band."

"You quit?"

Nicky shrugged. "I meant to come and tell you about that guy."

"D'you know my car?" Mack said. "You know I love my car. The day I buy it, and I saved for a long, long time, I say a prayer of thanks and I push the cross pin through the steering wheel. It's a dedication. It's a sign I'm ready to serve and to use all I have to serve. Then I see you, bud, up there, trashing your drums."

"They weren't my drums."

"Following that Sid boy. Buying into his whole thing." He pointed his mug and said, "I'm telling you now. It doesn't get any easier. Take it from one who knows."

Nicky sighed.

Mack raised his voice, "God gave you this gift. Look what you've done with it."

"Can I tell you about Danny Donnelly?"

He banged his mug down and the toaster popped, charcoaled toast smoking from the slots. A smoke detector went off.

Nicky shouted over the top. "I'm not finished putting the kit away. I need to go."

Mack was fanning a hand over the toaster, face screwed against the screeching alarm. Smoke spewed out.

"He's mental. His whole family."

Mack was wafting a folded magazine.

"Thought I should tell you. Just in case."

The bathroom door was open at the end of the hallway. He went in. The door was stiff, catching on the wiry carpet. It wouldn't close. He unzipped and aimed down the toilet, ringed with dust and loose pubes. In the hallway the alarm still blared and he heard the front door open and shut. He finished, shook off and did up his fly and washed his hands in the sink, caked with toothpaste blobs. The alarm kept going.

He took a quick glance along the hallway. Ruth was there, in a long skirt and a denim jacket. She faced the kitchen. All you could see was Mack's arm, sticking out the door. She had his fist in both hands. She held it close to her lips, brushing a thumb across the top.

"You're still here?" Mack said. His head had dipped over hers.

She turned. She dropped his hand.

Nicky went to speak then pointed at the bathroom. It was only a few steps and he was out the flat and in the close. He took the stairs two at a time, ears ringing.

Papers

Pete was climbing to his front door. He saw him through the glass and waited for the knock.

"I'm supposed to help you with the papers," he said. "My mum phoned yours."

"Yeah. I heard."

They went down the hill. They had to collect the load of papers from the newsagents.

"We might get soaked. You got a jacket?"

Pete shrugged. He pulled his sleeves over his hands and hunched his shoulders.

"Where's your new one?"

"They confiscated it. Said they were taking it back to the shop. But it's gubbed. Fag burns. Bastards'll probably fling it in the charity."

Once they were loaded up with papers they started on the main road. Houses there sat high above sloped gardens, steep concrete staircases leading to the doors. He gave Pete a bundle and sent him over to the odd numbers. He carried the pouch and did the evens. When Pete was finished he came across for more. Nicky told him he had to quit skipping over the fences.

"You have to go up and down every bloody one?"

"They complain."

"Stuck up arseholes."

Pete took a shot of the bag. They turned off the main road and walked down the spiral then cut through the lane to the dead end. Pete said they should deliver on the way down and walk back with a lighter bag but Pete didn't know. The shortcut wouldn't work that way.

They started at the dead end. The houses lined one side of the street with a railway line on the verge opposite. Pete had to stop and switch shoulders.

"Want me to take it back?" Nicky said.

"How much d'you get for this?"

He told him.

"That's shit. Pure slave labour. You should go on strike."

Nicky flipped the letterbox, took the paper and shoved it through.

"My brother worked at the bakery for a bit," Pete said. "They went on strike when some guy got fired for crashing a forklift. Turned out he'd been driving it pished, so it was pointless."

Folk on this street were decent so they stepped over the fence into the next garden. There was a fat black and white cat waiting in the porch.

"Watch," Nicky said. He took the paper and stuck an end through and the cat swiped for it. He dragged it out again. The cat crouched, eyes on the letterbox. He stuck the paper through slowly and the cat got on two feet and started flailing with both sets of claws, shredding as Nicky fed it in. The paper fell, flapping open and tenting over the cat's face. It flung it off, pounced and carried on shredding.

Pete laughed.

"You know that French teacher Fat Jacques. That's his house."

Pete laughed again. "Le chat de Fat Jacques. It's a mental wee bastard."

They watched while it tore the paper to confetti.

A few houses along Nicky said, "What d'you think Danny Donnelly'll do?"

"Says that guy's getting a kicking. Barry told him to tell the police. Get him done for hitting a minor."

"Think he will?"

"He's your mate that guy."

"Yeah. I know him."

"Danny Donnelly won't phone the pigs. Probably tell his dad and his brothers. Dunno what's worse."

Back on the main road, they went to the news-agents for the second lot. Pete bought himself a roll and crisps.

Blocks of flats stood across from the grass pitches. They were packed with old people. You had to climb to the top first and stuff your papers through on the way back down. If you weren't fast enough they'd hear their letterbox rattle, come out and trap you in long conversations about the weather or pets or paper rounds they had when they were a boy.

He jogged out the last block puffing and sweating.

Pete waited, munching his roll. "What took you?" he said.

"How come you got done so fast?"

"Just dumped them at the bottom of the stairs. They can take it if they want."

Nicky shook his head. "You need to post them."

"Who gives a fuck about it anyway?" Pete unfolded a copy and read the front. "*Burst Pipe Brings Mystery.* What a lot of shite." The rain had started. He watched wet dots appear on the paper and looked at the sky and said, "Let's take a break man. It'll be sheltered down the river."

They went through the bushes, down the broken wooden stairs and sat on the flat rock, water dripping off branches. Pete took a handful from the dusty bank and chucked it into the brown river. He wiped his hand on his jeans and nodded at the wee cliff on the other side. "Mind that time everyone was jumping off there. You were too chicken shit."

"You didn't either."

"Aye I did."

"You said if we swallowed any water we'd get dysentery."

"Bollocks," Pete said, bringing out a crumpled fag packet.

"Manage to get some fags in the end?"

He shook his head. "Aye, thanks for that. Ended up getting me lifted."

"What?"

"I was pure steamin', man. Tried to get this big guy to go in, then the pigs pulled up. Ended up lifting me and taking me home. Folks went berserk."

"Sorry."

"Well. You're an arsehole."

"It wasn't my fault."

"Doesn't mean you're not an arsehole."

Nicky looked away from him.

"You are. It's the truth."

"So are you."

"We're a pair of arseholes."

He smoked through tight lips. The braces had changed his face, made him thicker around the mouth. "I'm grounded. Forever fuckin' more. This is my last fag, so looks like I'll be quitting."

"Purdy must owe you some. All that lot."

Pete spat, kicked grey sand over the dark patch. "My brother got us the booze the other night. And all the nights before. I'm a silly prick – during the shitstorm I ended up grassing him in to my folks. He's fuckin' raging. They're fuckin' raging." He sighed. "Danny Donnelly'll still want me to get the drink but I can't. I was getting Jennifer Black's n'all."

"Might make life easier."

"Thanks for telling her about me shiteing myself by the way."

Nicky stared over the water.

"You said you wouldn't tell anyone," Pete said.

"It was years ago."

"You told me you wouldn't say anything about it, ever."

Nicky shrugged. "Sorry."

Pete blew smoke at the ground. His face broke into a grin. "I don't give a shit anyway. I pulled her."

"No you didn't."

"Aye I did."

"Don't believe you."

"Don't care. It happened man. And not just that."

The shower passed and the circles on the brown surface turned to pinpricks then the water smoothed. Following it along eventually led you to the big waterfall, where the river churned into rank foam and spat faded litter on the rocks and branches at the bottom. Sometimes there was a heron, standing skinny and grey and watching with a yellow eye.

Nicky said, "I had some joy too."

Pete was savouring his fag, studying it between draws. He turned. "One of the mosher girls? Was it the big Nazi Witch?"

"She wanted to. I gave her the K.B."

Pete laughed. "Yeah. Sure. If she's that desperate mibbe I should have a word."

"She likes deflowering young virgins."

"I'll be no use then."

Pete smoked. He had about an inch of cigarette left. He watched it burn again.

Smoke

The coffin sat lid shut between velvet curtains, the wood a deep brown colour, almost red with a brass bar running across the side. He was late. In the wee entrance hall the minister's voice droned low. Nicky peered through the door, waiting for the next hymn. The minister stood at a lectern to the side of the coffin, hands together in a steeple. There was a long pause, his mouth a grim line. He said a few more words and then the line twisted into a sad smile and quiet laughter went around the hall.

Someone hissed. A janitor had been shuffling about earlier but was in the service now, tucked at a side door in blue overalls with his head bowed. The hiss came again. Nicky looked over his shoulder. Sid peered in from outside. His hair was washed, the long strip lying flat and soft down the middle.

They stood in the garden, trees around the building bare with branches jagging at the sky. Sid was in school trousers and an old blazer, a pale patch where the school's badge had been unstitched from the pocket. Both of them wore black ties.

"Should you not be in there?" Nicky said.

"I told them I couldn't deal with it man. When we got here we had to queue. Against that wall there, watching this other miserable mob file out. There was smoke coming out there," he nodded at the high chimney, "stank man. Fuckin' stank."

"Are you awright? I'm sorry about—"

"Aye. You kidding? I just said it to get out the thing. Who wants to sit through that shitey festival of woe." Sid turned and looked down the winding drive. He sniffed. Two long black cars were parked, wheels on the kerb.

"I'm sorry about your Grandpa," Nicky said.

"Today was the first time I got a shot in a limousine. Pure let down. No tellies or sliding screens or anything. Ever since I seen that bit in Home Alone 2 I've been wanting a go in one." He felt his ear where the earring had been taken out. The blazer was too wee and rode up to his elbows when he bent them

"Sure we shouldn't go in?" Nicky said.

"No chance. How come you're here anyway?"

"Just thought I should come."

"Where'd you get that massive suit?"

"Borrowed it."

"You're missing school but."

Nicky shrugged.

"Fuck sake Messiah."

"What?"

"Skiving school to go to some fuckin' funeral of an old guy you don't even know?" He sucked in the last of the fag, laughing smoke out his nostrils.

"I did know him. I went to see him once."

"How?"

"The guy Mack took me to the old folks' home to meet him."

"The guy who went and punched that big scary bastard?"

"Yeah."

"Is he a weirdo?"

"He's awright."

"It's horrible that place. Pure roasting all year round. And reeks of pish. Imagine that's where you got left to fuckin' expire. I never went."

Sid got a second fag going and they moved round the side of the building and sat on a bench. Frost prickled between the slats and numbed their arses. A wee brass plaque was screwed in the middle. *In memory of J. Clarence*, it said. Sid glanced at him and leaned forward, elbows on knees. He sighed. Magpies were hopping around the patch of grass in front of them.

"What's your mum saying about the guitar?"

"She's not noticed. The house's been full of all these fuckin' cousins and great uncles I've never even seen before. Think I should tell her? Might be a good time, since it's not as bad as her dad being dead."

"What about practises?"

Sid stretched his legs out, crossed at the ankles. "Look at these shoes man." It was the old black slip-ons, the pair he'd hidden the video under. His head rolled back at the sky.

"We can't practise if you've no guitar."

"True."

Nicky tucked his hands in his sleeves and folded them under his armpits. "Fadge said I'm getting kicked out."

"Did he?"

"Said he spoke to you."

"What's the point in kicking you out?"

"I dunno what I did to him."

"If I don't have a guitar we can't practise or do gigs, so there is no Fuck Trumpets. There's nothing to kick you out off."

"Someone could lend you one."

"Mibbe."

"I know some folk. Want me to ask about?"

Sid sighed and uncrossed his legs. "You kind of fucked it, Messiah. He hates your guts."

Nicky unbuttoned the suit jacket and wrapped it tighter around himself.

"Young MacFadgen," Sid said. "Fadge goes on like he hates her, but he hates it even more when she's getting some action."

"We didn't do anything."

"That's not what I heard. Not what folk are saying. Glove called it the second coming. Funny wee bastard."

Nicky swallowed.

Sid straightened in the seat. "You're going pure red man. Did that actually fuckin' happen?"

Nicky shrugged.

"You shagged her?"

He shook his head. "No."

"So why d'you look guilty as hell?"

"Nothing. I just went round to see her."

"Hand job?"

Nicky shook his head.

"Feed the horse?"

He shook it again.

Sid slid along and their shoulders pressed. "You're a shit liar son. Something happened."

"I just got off with her."

"And that's it?"

He shrugged. "On her bed."

"Just pure kissing?"

"For ages."

"Where'd she let you touch?"

"I dunno. Her back."

"Her back?"

"Yeah. It was nice. Soft."

Sid sat grinning at him, the deep dimples appearing like brackets round his mouth.

"Did she make you cream yourself?"

An organ started groaning from the building, faintly through the bricks, but even outside but you could hear the terrible sound of it. No one was singing. There were no words. Sid's face fell and he stiffened and Nicky's hands clenched. Notes curdled and droned on and on. The magpies took off. Sid sniffed and ground the fag end into the arm of the bench, leaving it standing in a ring of ash. The organ finished.

"Don't tell anyone," Nicky said.

"Course I won't, man."

They were silent for a second, sniffing the air.

"What'll you do, without drums?"

"Same as I'll do without my guitar. Fuck all."

"Me and you could do something. Fadge's always getting it wrong anyway. He's—"

"It's done man. The Fuck Trumpets is done."

New cars appeared at the foot of the driveway.

"They'll be out soon," Sid said.

"I should go then."

"Stay a bit, Messiah. Do your bit for mankind."

Their shoulders still touched. Nicky turned and Sid sat with his eyes on the chimney, waiting.